Bludgeoned Girls Press Presents...

Prolonged Torments Bound in the Worst of Evils

By Anton Cancre

Copyright 2024 Anton Cancre

All rights reserved. No portion of this book may be reproduced in any form without permission from the author or publisher, except as permitted by U.S. copywrite law.

Cover art by Betty Rocksteady

Table of Contents

Introduction	07
In the Muck Writhes Hope	09
Endless, He Said	15
By Silken Strings, Tied	35
When the Moon Sighs Solitude	39
Beings in Empty: a Haibun	61
Under the Pretext of Propensity	65
The Glorious Adventure of The Premiere Size Queen of The Appalachian Trail Inside a Positively Gargantuan Cunt	89
Interchangeable Parts	107
Self-Fulfilling Prophecies Always Reveal Themselves in the Shittiest of Bars	123
What They Don't Tell You About the Mummy's Curse	131
Violence Works in Mysterious Ways	141
Professional Development	165
Debts of Generations Past, Come Due	171

If You Were Dreaming, You'd Know	187
What Grows Inside	193
One Time Would Be Enough	217
Jesus of Jim Beam	223
On the Frustrations of Modern Wendigos	231
Beautiful Things	237
She Stalks These Streets as Her Own Forest	261
Blood In, Blood Out	267
The Devil's Song	281
We've Lost that Wounded Look We Used to Have	289
When We Appear Before You Without Our Masks	295

Introduction

Prepare yourself.

What you're about to read are not the stories you might expect from Anton Cancre. Anton is easily the kindest, gentlest, most compassionate person I've ever met. He teaches kids in prison, for Pete's sake. He has more love in his heart than anyone should be able to reasonably hold.

But these stories are not that.

These are tales of bezoars and gristle wrapped in stinking entrails. These are stories about the darkest, most depraved horrors the human mind can conjure, the terrors we dare not think about, the madness that threatens to transform us into our most violent impulses.

It's all described in the most delicate, precise poetry, and the characters seem so very real, as if each story could be told to you by a person sitting on the stool beside you in some seedy dive bar. These are mesmerizing tales, startling in their beauty, growing more and more disturbing as they blossom into something huge and wretched and corpse-scented.

So, prepare yourself. Prepare to be aroused, amused, disgusted, disturbed, and horrified. Learn what it's like to fuck a mummy or climb inside the vagina of a giant woman. Find out why spiders make their human puppets dance. Take vengeance on cruel fathers, pedo stepfathers, and creeps in bars. Taste another man's sin. Let the Tillinghast Resonator change you forever. Birth something unspeakable.

These horrors and many more await you in these pages. Every detail is described so that your senses will be absorbed completely into the story, even when you'd rather they weren't, even when your mind starts to fracture and resist the pull of these horrors, the tastes and sights and sounds too much to bear.

    Don't say I didn't warn you.

    -Sarah Hans "Author of Asylum and A Chorus of Whispers"

In the Muck Writhes Hope

They always said to stay clear of that stretch of beach, that stretch of shore, that stretch of whatever you would call this particular fifty meters of sticky mud run through with the twisting, angry barbs of old mangrove roots. The brackish water reached about waist high and the only things one was likely to feel around their ankles and legs was the tentative brushes and curious nibbles of whatever lived there. Not exactly the kind of place your average teen longed to spend their precious unobserved nocturnal hours.

Denial, though. Well, denial can be a siren call of its own. The lure of the unknown. The forbidden. Such things are the nectar of youth. Why else would so many of us have lurked our way through abandoned construction sites and dilapidated buildings whose floorboards have gone squishy with rot?

Why else would little Netty Thurnbirge have been on that specific bit of beach in the depths of night? Her tangled lanks of neon red tentacles, wet and dripping from the humidity, sticking to her face as she forced her old Converse down into and up out of the muck. Knowing better didn't force away the bone deep certainty in the back of her brain that she was back in those septic pits, up to her knees down to her shoulders in strangers' shit as she snaked out the mummified remains of yet another dead possum.

The heavy, sweet reek of decay and detritus didn't do much to shirk the mental image. Hell, she'd been sure enough of strange forms wriggling their way through and around her legs back then as well, feasting on the digestive castoffs of those too good to deal with their own waste.

Just another drudge to trudge through. She could keep going if she could keep it to that. There were things under the black water where moon and starlight didn't reach, but they gave less of a shit about her than those same stars and that same damn moon. Abominations never wasted their efforts on other abominations.

She kept hearing his voice. Not on the breeze. No. Never on the breeze, nor echoing through cheap aluminum walls ever again. Her old boy scout knife, oiled to the bright white of God itself and run over a spit-slick stone until the edge could split atoms, saw to that. He didn't even scream.

After all that bluster, years of flexed muscles, midnight screeds, and bared teeth and tensed knuckles, no more than a feeble gurgle of crimson escaped the thin, deep line she had drawn across his throat. Maybe he'd even been proud of how cleanly she'd severed the carotids.

Still, she heard it. Nothing more than her name. Likely nothing more than the wind, but it sounded the same. That heavy, intentionally enunciated "d" and the vicious, angry intent it held. The same stress she put on the double "t" as he slipped to the floor in their barely standing, certainly-not-mobile home. Well after any pretense of strength had left him but before the glint of understanding left his eyes. When she'd dug bare handed into his abdomen. Clawing with ragged, chewed nails through the pale flesh of his stomach. Skin peeling away in rough strips over the loose, greasy lumps of fat beneath.

She was surprised at how dense the muscle beneath the thick layers of fat was. Too many evenings sucking down drive-through delights without a single sit-up in between led her to expect maybe a paper-thin layer of red roped protein strands layered with thick tendrils of tendon.

Her detached, cold evaluation shocked her more than anything else. The realization that she would need to go back to using the knife if she wanted it to be quick enough for him to see her work and the red eyed, screaming rage that propelled it. The evaluation of pupil dilation and mental math of shock settling in to numb nerve endings.

Convulsions shook his body as she split his abdominal wall cleanly along the tendon lines. Not fighting the grain of the muscles but working with it. Just like dear old dad taught her on all those hunting trips he was sure would knock *this stupid phase* loose. She slipped her hands into the slit, grabbing the slippery blue-grey ropes and yanking them into the light.

She needed him to see.

See how full of shit he was. How little his own self-righteousness meant once he was reduced to unprocessed sausage. See how little his rants and rage meant to the world.

No. What she heard was inside her own head, the last remnants of a morality forced upon her trying to claw their way back inside. There were far more important voices to listen to now. The ones Old Myrtle had told her to be wary of. Well-meaning enough, and certainly nicer about it than dear old dad, Myrtle had intended the stories to be a warning. A way of keeping her on the well-trod path. Keeping her safe in the only way old Myrtle thought safety could exist. Even when tears clearly shown in the corners of her eyes and the purple black blood welled just beneath the surface of her skin.

No words. An ebb and flow, to be sure. But no words.

Sounds felt inside her skull. Vibrations pulsing their way out from the center of her being. Pulling her forward. Subtle suggestions to slip her feet from the thinning canvas and worn rubber. To dig her toes into the layers of mud. To feel the undulations of thick, meaty tongues of tiny clams lapping against the calluses of her feet. Wearing them down to bare skin. Soft. Supple. Gentle as the wet rot they slipped through.

Crabs scuttling along calves and thighs. Nimble claws picking at old skin. Pulling it into mandibles that shredded it further before devouring.

Slow fish nipping and nibbling and the somehow wetter than water mucus of leeches inching their way along her skin in search of a fresh vein to pop. A wholesale devouring of what she had been in favor of the new form that awaited her beneath the waves.

Endless, He Said

Images began to form behind his eyes. Not in flashes or floods, but a sludge-slow trickle. Chemicals leaking from dendrite to dendrite, swimming lazily through the gaps between neurons. Disparate pieces of a jumbled puzzle linking in random locations.

Red. Bright. Too much. Over everything. Drowning the room. The world. Filling him. Leeching his life.

Then black. Seeping in.

Eyelids heavy, he forced them open. The room was a blur of colors and shapes. Angry, painful light burst through open curtains

Someone didn't like those curtains. Bright. Busy. Too grandma. Who? Couldn't remember.

Something grey. Pale. Limp and crumpled in on itself. Laying under the window. In the shadow. Too close to that misshaped black lump. Too close to the puddle of pink. He didn't like that lump, so he looked away from it.

The Lump was bad. He didn't like looking at it. His neck popped and groaned as he turned toward anything else.

The soft, round, brown, and oblong shape had to be the couch. It wrapped around him. Cradled him. He wanted to feel comforted, but something jabbed at his mind like a thorn. Something was wrong.

It was supposed to be white. There had been arguments. Something about stains and cleaning. Someone was a sloppy little pig.

He knew he should get up. He wanted to. He needed to do something. Maybe hunger? His stomach wasn't growling but he felt empty. There was food somewhere in the house. There had to be. All he had to do was get up.

A small thing. Stand up. Walk. Defy gravity. Coordinate hundreds of strands of muscles and ligaments. Put one foot in front of the other without falling over somehow.
The thought exhausted him.

His neck ached. Not screaming agony, but insistent. A steady moan buzz of angry nerves. He could lift his arm to check on it. That much was possible. It had to be.

The muscles were stiff and sore, but they complied. His

hand rose slowly. Eventually, it reached the source of the ache. He expected pain. The bright jolt of a poked bruise. Instead, there was nothing. Not just a lack of pain. Nothing at all. An absence where the skin of his neck should have been. Raw, cold meat on deeper probing. Still no real pain. Not the agony an open wound should give.

There were teeth. Dull green eyes that should have shone like emeralds, staring from beneath black felt. Grey hands grabbing him like steel claws. His pain rested on the edges of those teeth and in the emptiness of that gaze.

He remembered weight, too. Cold, blunt steel in his hand. The momentum and the crunch of cracked skull that made his stomach lurch. Over and over until the hands let go and the teeth and the eyes fell away. Then the red came.

* * *

"You know what they said," Hunter said.
"Yeah," Jade replied. Short and stern with those deep green eyes boring holes through him. "Buncha face-flapping toadies paid to keep us all terrified. Locked in our homes and under control. You

damn well know better than to fall for that bullshit."

His pale, rail thin arms were flailing as he spoke, building up momentum for the soapbox. A pastor psyching himself up for the choir. He hadn't hit his stride yet, but Hunter knew he was saving that for the pulpit. He couldn't help wondering if the ashes from the end of Jade's cigarette were going to catch on the carpet. Then they'd both have no choice but to break curfew and to be out there.

In the street.

"I know it sounds crazy."

Hunter was trying to keep his voice even. Concentrating on the rhythm of the words and keeping them measured.

"There's no reason to believe a word of it. I get it."

He took a breath, looking Jade directly in the eyes.

"But you weren't there when it happened. You didn't see them all together. YOU didn't feel how still the air got. Didn't watch what they... I..." Hunter trailed off; his tongue frozen in his mouth. Words lost form in the images and his mind stopped dead.

"You saw people acting up and acting out."

There it was. The cherry of that damn cigarette pointed right at him. There might be no congregation, but it was still time for Jade to preach.

"You saw people that finally had enough of this bullshit. You saw people who realized there was no way out. You saw people with no other options left. YOU saw them stand up and lash out for a change."

That silly goddamn night-black bowler with the sillier pink ribbons hanging off the brim was bouncing around on his head. It would have been funny without sound; so much fury and flurry of motion. Jade always tended toward the dramatic and he became a tornado when he was passionate.

"It's what we've always dreamed of, happening right in front of us. All around us. How many times did you scream at the TV that we needed to burn the whole thing down? The match has finally been lit.

"It's happening on our own doorstep. You were there when the flame hit the floor. You were there and YOU could have doused the place with gasoline. Instead, you cowered, with your tail between your legs."

Jade's hand was on the doorknob. His cigarette trailed smoke. Hunter knew he should say something, kiss him deeply, or punch him in the jaw. He knew he should scream at Jade about the all too real blood in the streets. His lungs froze in his chest, lips stone.

* * *

Time passed. The shadows were longer or deeper. Maybe there were just more of them.

Had he slept? He didn't remember losing consciousness. He didn't remember much of anything. Maybe the shadows were always this dark. He wanted them to back off and give him space. Maybe he dreamt they were shorter before, back when he was…

The thought slipped through his fingers. He waved them in front of his head, trying to grab it before it disappeared. They were too stiff, too clumsy and too slow. It passed away into nothing.

Food.

That's what he needed. Something solid and substantial that would sit in his stomach like a rock. He wasn't supposed to be eating red meat. Reasons and attendant arguments hid in the muck of his memories, but they didn't matter. A steak would do the trick. Rare and bleeding. Then he could think straight.

But the floor was so... comfortable didn't seem like the right word. His back was sore and stiff. His ass felt flat and swollen. It felt like something was moving underneath his thighs.

Maybe comforting. It was solid. Stable. So much better than the couch he had slid off. It didn't reach out to smother him like the damnable black fingers reaching out from the corners. It didn't ooze out from under him like every thought while he tried to make sense of himself. The floor was there. It had always been there. The floor would always be there.
Endlessly unchanging.

* * *

It was the same on both of their shirts. Stark red on white cotton in gorgeous, delicate script. The back told a different story. Simple block lettering, bold and invasive. The alternating colors of the rainbow blending smoothly: SSDD. Resting atop a single coil of deep brown, piled pyramid-like to give the impression of concentric circles. An inwardly spiraling cone spotted with yellow.

Hunter caught those green eyes fluttering over to his several times over the night. Quick, like squirrels jetting after a stray nut, but noticeable. Hunter couldn't bring himself to go over though. His mouth turned into a wadded mass of cotton whenever he considered it. The room was too small. The stark white walls with those garish thick pink stripes slashing across them closed in around him. There were too few people to hide among them and everywhere he went those eyes were there, peeking out from behind a swoop of black hair.

There wasn't enough liquor to loosen his tongue or to pry his feet from their spot, cemented into the floorboards. He could drown his liver in vodka and gin and still never have enough to move. What would he say if he did? Some foolish pick-up line?

Come here often?

Was your father a thief?

Those pants are fabulous, but they'd look better on my floor.

How quickly would those full, round lips turn sharp if he did? What fire would spill from between them and leave him smoldering in a pile of ash? Any amount of self-hatred he was guaranteed to feel in the morning had to be better than that.

In the end, the decision was made for him.

Shouting. A thin, black cigarette punctuated each bellow with a thrust. The cherry getting closer and closer to the other man's face. The words, and any sense they may have held, were lost in the thunder. The other one looked like a friend of Nixon's, who had a thing for muscle-bound giants. A sense of righteousness, no matter how well earned, and a tiny bit of flame wouldn't stand a chance where this was headed.

Hunter didn't think about what he was doing. His feet moved on their own, striding with purpose. His left hand reached out, snatched the cigarette mid thrust and dunked it into his drink. It was a waste of good vodka, but the insistent hiss silenced the room.

"These kids today," the words flowed smoothly off his tongue, as if coming from someone else. "All hopped up on the cloves and starting shit with houseplants."

His right hand pressed firmly on the back. Bone jutted sharp beneath trembling skin. There was pressure. Turning. A slight nod to the host.

"It was a lovely evening," Hunter said to no one in particular, "but I think we'd better get to rehab before he burns the whole house to cinders."

The door opened.

"Nice shirt," Jade said as they stepped into the night together.

* * *

The sun was in his eyes. It moved. He had to think to blink, concentrate on making the muscles move to make it a reality. The sound they made, a soft rasp, as they scraped across his eyes worried him. The sunlight, harsh as it was, failed to bother him as much as the nagging thought that something wasn't right.

Something was supposed to be there, blocking the light. Blocking THEM. Something important.

Something to keep him. No, not him. Them. Something to keep them both safe.

Something that didn't work.

He wanted to do something about it. The boards were right there, next to the grey lump on the floor beneath the window. The hammer had to be nearby. There must be nails somewhere. His legs didn't feel so stiff anymore. An easy, quick task...

It would still be there later, though. The damage was done. No point in worrying about it now. Besides, he might come home soon.

* * *

Another day done and Hunter was on his way home. Usually, there wasn't much traffic this late. One of the few perks of working retail; selling the same fucking print of the same fucking flowers to the same fucking idiots to hang over the same fucking table in their dining room. But the later shifts meant sleeping in later and that he didn't have to deal with the traffic jams everyone else complained about. It was usually smooth sailing coming in and going home.

Tonight was different. Likely, some asshole jumped the gun on a light and everyone was gawking. The radio was off, an old bastard with a tape deck and an older Erasure tape stuck in it. The choice was Ship of Fools or nothing, so he chose nothing. His half blown out speakers wouldn't have been able to cover the cacophony of blaring horns and curses being hurled around anyways.

At least the air conditioner worked, so he could keep the windows up. There was too much exhaust built up from all the cars sitting stagnate and the buildings crammed on top of each other over the street kept the wind from blowing it away. He coughed enough from the clove smoke in the house, he didn't need to do any more damage to his lungs.

A woman walked along the sidewalk toward his car, slouching wearily, as if toward Bethlehem. From the matted brown dirt in her hair and the torn, stained clothes, he assumed she was homeless.

"Just walk on by," he mumbled to himself, hoping the words would work. "Think I'd drive a piece of shit like this if I had any money?"

They didn't. She didn't. She came right up to the passenger side window, pawing at the glass like a cat begging to come in. Her hand left thick streaks of crimson down the glass. He worried that it might not be mud all over her, but there was nothing he could do to help.

I'm not a damn doctor, he thought.

She wasn't taking the hint, so he gave up trying to pretend he didn't notice her. Her jaw worked in slow, steady circles. She was looking him dead in the eye. Her left fist began pounding on the glass, while her right was still sliding and scraping at the window. It was too much for him to handle.

"Look," Hunter screamed, "I don't ha-"

There was a sharp crack, like thunder. An explosion of red, grey, and white burst across the window. He thought he heard a faint thump on the ground outside the door. There was more thunder rolling down the street and out from the alleys.

He looked out through the windshield but couldn't make sense of what he saw. It was all too far removed from prior experience and context. Olive green and khaki figures swarmed across the road. Rifles held ready in their hands, muzzles flashing noon sun white. People, just regular people in severe black and white business suits and bright green house dresses were everywhere now. Just walking through it all. Every once and a while, one would jerk once or twice and fall to the ground.

One of the soldiers was in the middle of a group. Close enough that Hunter could hear the curses he yelled between shots fired. Most of the people around him dropped, but not all. They were moving in closer. Hunter didn't see any weapons. They didn't seem to be yelling or showing any of the usual signs of anger. Just walking toward him slowly, methodically. Two reached him from behind and grabbed him by the shoulders, pulling him to the ground. Shouts turned to screams, screams to undefined vowels. Vowels drawn out until they finally disappeared.

Someone stepped out of the car in front of him. A woman in a slinky blue dress and three-inch heels. Hunter couldn't make out what she said, but she shouted whatever it was. Her head flew back and forth as she strode over to a teenager with bright blue hair and shredded jeans. His back was to Hunter, but he must have said something, done something. The bright red rage drained from her face; her hands dropped to her sides. She started to back away from him. Her foot must've caught on a rock or something, because she tumbled down backwards. With the racket of the air conditioner blocking out the sound from outside, it was almost funny. All that self-possessed, entitled anger turning to fear and a well-deserved slip on the pavement. The terror on her face was too clear, even from a distance. Eyes wide as she frantically pulled herself up. She was nearly standing when the teenager reached her.

Hunter expected blows to fall. Punches. Kicks. Maybe some spitting. The usual street fight stuff. He didn't expect the teen to lunge in, face first and mouth agape. Didn't expect to see teeth clamp down on the flesh of the forearm she threw up in front of her face and continue forcing their way through skin and muscle. He'd been bitten before, once by a pissed off dog and again by an even more pissed off eight-year-old. The dog left some punctures in the skin and both incidents bruised his muscles all to hell. The pain was terrible, but neither of them tore anything loose. He flinched in sympathetic agony and watched her scream into the sky, slapping and pushing at the teen with her other hand. The teen finally released her with a backwards yank that tore the last strings of skin, muscle and tendon free. Blood ran down from the wound. She tried to turn, probably to run back to the relative safety of her car, but he lunged at her again, throwing both of them to the ground.

    Hunter couldn't handle any more. The confusion, the fear, and the impotent anger overwhelmed him. His lizard brain took over. Conscious thought was shut down. He crawled into the back seat and pulled the emergency thermal blanket over top of him. Curled up in a ball, he whimpered softly to block out the sound of the screams and the shots being fired.

* * *

Something small, gray, and furry pulled on his little toe. Somehow, he didn't notice it chewing through his shoe. Now it was gnawing on HIM. A dim memory expected pain or shock or anger. There was nothing. He should be swatting at it. Screaming and kicking and stomping. He couldn't bring himself to stand up and just stared.

He thought about how warm it must be. Pulsing with blood and meat. Wriggling. Squealing.

His arm acted on its own, grabbing the rat before he was sure what it was doing. The expected squeals came. It fought back against his grip. Tiny claws shredded the skin of his fingers. Teeth sunk into his knuckle. Warm, yellow liquid spilled down over his hand. His grip didn't loosen. When he pulled it to his mouth, his teeth and jaws did their work. Clamping down. Crushing small, brittle bones, and tearing through both fur and skin.

The squeals stopped. Then the wriggling. His tongue pushed warm, wet meat down his throat to fill the empty pit inside him.

The rest of the bites were easier. Less fight meant less work. The skin was tough, the meat stringy. Fur didn't catch in his throat quite the way he expected it would. He pounded its head against the floor to free its brain from the cage of its skull. In the end, he ended up chewing the remaining fragments of bone anyways.

His clothes were a mess. The volume of blood in something that small surprised him. It was everywhere. Flies were already settling on his shirt. The yawning gulf in him didn't feel any fuller.

* * *

"They consider it a delicacy there," Jade said, a smile stretching his lips to thin crescents, "Starch said so."

He was seated across the small, plastic kitchen table, picking at the remains of a chicken leg on his plate. Those thin, dexterous fingers snatched little morsels of meat from the crooks of gristle and bone. They were greasy, shining orange and yellow in the light of the single candle. With each bite he would slide them part of the way into his mouth, sucking at their tips. The seduction wasn't subtle. Nothing Jade did was subtle. At the same time, Hunter was mesmerized.

"I think it's a given," Hunter said, trying to keep his focus, "that anything people cook on the street isn't a delicacy. Sounds more like a quick way to contract every foodborne illness on the face of the planet. That's the type of thing people only eat when they have no choice, or if they're tourists."

He forced a laugh and half-heartedly tossed a kernel of corn at Jade, who ducked aside with a dramatic flourish. Every moment was a show for him.

"But that's why I'll have to eat it," he said. "It's part of the experience, both good and bad. You're just scared I'll like it. That I'll come back demanding rat kebab every night and you'll have to find some dark stall at the farmer's market where they are willing to admit what the pale, shaved meat actually is. Or that I won't be able to leave the convenience of charred rodent, grilled to order right on every corner."

The last bit hit a little too hard. The façade slipped a little. Hunter's eyes dropped to his plate, to his own trembling hands. His breath caught in his chest. The laughter choked off.

"Shit," Jade said, taking hold of Hunter's hands. The grease smeared tracks along them. "You know I don't mean that. Six months is a damn long time. It'll be hard on me too, but I don't have a choice about it."

Jade lifted Hunter's hands and placed them against his cheeks. He stroked them down along the soft fuzz. At twenty-three, he still couldn't grow a proper beard. It was a bit of a joke between them, that he was trapped at prepubescence. An eternal teenager that would never get to be an adult, like Peter Pan. The sensation soothed Hunter, even as his heart beat faster. Hunter's breathing calmed and the trembling stopped.

"I have a plane to catch in the morning, but we still have tonight. Let's not ruin it by getting all weepy." Jade stood up and walked around the table without releasing his grip on Hunter's hands, even when they passed over the candle's flame. "Besides, I know you'll wait for me. 'Until the world burns and the roads go silent. Until the last of us shuffles off into oblivion. Endlessly.' Isn't that how you put it?"

* * *

The sun was in his eyes again. Not as strong this time. Filtered and gray in smoke that wafted lazily through the remains of the window. The last of the screams died out last night. Or last week. The memories were fading again, getting tougher to hold onto. Everything was blurring.

He knew he ate something at some point. A feather was stuck in his teeth. Something black and loud had pecked at his tongue. He bit its head off when it thought it was getting an easy meal. There was no point in going out to hunt, not when food brought itself to him.

He was comfortable here. As comfortable as he could be, at least, with tendons drying out and tightening. In his spot against the wall, he could see the door, the window, and that crumpled form beneath it. Flesh too far gone to be any good to him. If someone were to come in, he'd know. He'd be ready.

He had to wait. Some part of him knew, somehow, that it was important to stay here and stay vigilant. A name danced on the tip of remembrance. It wouldn't sit still. Wouldn't let him grasp it. But it mattered. More than the smoke or the gaping emptiness inside, it mattered. And he had all the time in the world.

By Silken Strings, Tied

"They just pull them out of their asses, you know," Eunice whispered out of the side of her mouth. "Then yank us around, dancing to whatever tune they choose."

Aicha didn't say anything, just let her body move with the directed sways. It was too easy to talk of the arbitrary nature of control as if something new was being said. Of course, power was arbitrary. Fickle and unconnected to any greater meaning or purpose.

In some other world, some other reality, she'd be chasing them into corners with a rolled-up paper or the flat end of a fancy shoe. Flattening chitinous bodies and spreading the protected organs like paste. Or, if feeling more magnanimous, she could pick them up by their fragile threads and carry them out into the sun. They would likely be eaten by some bird, but the blood wouldn't be on her hands. It was a dream they'd all held.

But the spinnerets work, like tiny fingerbones, weaving the threads that tied her and her sisters to their fate. So fast and dexterous, they are. She used to think them beautiful. She used to think of all the things they could do with them.

She dreamt of beautiful homes, collecting the early morning dew on nearly invisible ties that swirled in and out of each other. Circles and spirals and funnels spinning tighter into each other. Later, these dreams twisted to images of wound, bound fools trapped and packaged for consumption.

All those dreams, even the ones of blood and bodies dissolving to viscous, fluid food, faded through the years. What could be done didn't matter in the face of what was done.

Yes, they had the tools to catch the sun in intricate whorls and knots, refracting the light in ways that would make the stars themselves jealous. But they chose to knit ropes. They chose to loop those ropes in tight knots around her wrists and those of her sisters. They chose to wave their multifarious limbs in intricate, inane movements that drug her own joints along for the ride.

It was insulting, moving in such stilted, mechanical motions. Being tied to these simplistic patterns when she could see so much more potential in the air and space around her. But no matter the idiocy of the situation, the situation still held sway. Whether or not she liked the dancing, the dancing would happen.

Eventually the dancing would not be so lonesome. The

whispering voices from above constantly chittered of descension. There would be glory and joy in intertwined clicking of hardened shells. In pedipalp insertion and transference of genetic material. The constrained and mechanical motions would come to their fruition then, some other set of arms moving hers in gentle gesticulations over the cephalothorax and abdomen of whoever or whatever had chosen her.

Her duty and purpose fulfilled, finally.

So, yes, this whole dance was absurd. As absurd as the giant teardrop pouch Wakamura carried on her abdomen as she continued to be jerked around in more and more frantic movements despite the strained and manic look that grew in her eyes. As absurd as the dynamic that had brought it all to bear.

But the absurdity didn't affect the reality of it. Eunice's great revelation that no divine hand guided coxa and claw changed nothing. It was just wind. The voices above had much to say on the effect of wind on the great ropes that guided eternity.

Still, as the rows of her eyes lit upon the smooth, hard surface of her own tarsus, flowing with the onyx glass bound by thin, pale cord, some deep forgotten voice echoed from the DNA of history. Speaking in images instead of words, she felt the weight of time radiating in red waves from her abdomen.

A competing voice from below, full of fangs. The sinking of chelicera through chitin and into the meat of the matter. A belly full from the descending and a pouch bloated with daughters who will not dance to any tune but their own

When the Moon Sighs Solitude

for Erin, may our fears stay just that.

I remember, or at least think I remember in whatever dim concept of memory I can still hold onto when the thoughts don't slip through my neurons like fine beach sand between my fingers, asking her if she would still love me when the chemical explosions stopped occurring in the right order.

When the cylinders in an engine stop firing in proper succession, a car ceases to be a car and becomes a shuddering, squealing, roaring weight that coughs out poison and takes up space without accomplishing anything. The past stops mattering in that moment. Saturday nights at the drive-in, with too many people crammed in and hollering over the two stuttering speakers that worked. Afternoons spent splitting knuckles on tacky bolts, hands coated in grit and grease amid fouled attempts to grasp the inner workings. Late night and early morning fumblings with cloth latches and soft flesh, mouths wet and sliding over each other under the dim green glow of the dashboard. Every bit of that gets shuffled aside when you call around to find the cheapest deal on getting it towed to the nearest junkyard.

She answered. I'm sure of it. She must have. I know. But the damn dog had started complaining about the stock market and those idiots that were running his portfolio into the ground and I couldn't concentrate when he got like that. He was just too loud for me to think straight.

Not that her answer, whatever it was, means much of anything anymore. Except for the times that I do, I don't blame her. Don't have the slightest clue where she stands on that. But I'm putting the cart before the horse a bit here, aren't I? You asked about the machine, about the treatments, and I'm rambling on about my burdens.

I get a little confused sometimes. Sequence becomes fuzzy and I wobble too much when I can't find the line. I'll try to walk it as best I can.

The machine. That damnable piece of whistling electrodes and beeping diodes. They called it a treatment. *Preventative measures through direct stimulation of the pineal.* That's what they told most of us, as if any of us had the slightest clue what it meant.

The dense terminology worked well enough to get them funding from the slimy faced paper pushers and slick-grinning number crunchers. Had to keep it all in the concrete with the greasy, doe-eyed and dull skulled company men.

I sat in on one of those meetings as their little show-pony. Shark-faced men and women in white smocks droning on and on about the decrease of melanin production with age and pineal calcification, listing data connecting them with Alzheimer's. Theoretical mumblings layered among thick Latin and Greek poured from their mouths onto the oak table and into the ears of powerful people who hadn't heard a lick of either language since their days in the frat or what the nuns shouted as they slapped their hands in Catholic school. All so official when paired with the charts and graphs of the only thing that really mattered in the conversation: potential profit margins.

Minds as sharp as their teeth, they didn't bother mentioning to those around the table what they'd told us in the quiet of their soft, pale rooms. They didn't say anything to the board about how the pineal gland sees the light. Locked deep in the black pits of our skulls, it still sees the light. Clicking off and on, like a switch turned on by the light, instead of the other way around. Nothing whatsoever about Descartes and the body as a "statue, or machine made of earth". Not a mention of the same man's belief in the role the pineal gland has in regards to sensation, imagination and, above all else, memory.

No, those selachian women and men piped their song in tune with the wants of suits and paper, and those ensconced in both danced in sync. Financial arteries were severed, and green rivers flowed from their gaping accounts. We rode the tide with no regrets.

If you like fishing, you should try the bays along the coast. It's beautiful country and you'll never go home with an empty cooler. The fish are drawn to the crab and lobster traps. To watch the dull witted, simple chitinous beasts crawl in after the tiniest morsel of rotting meat, so entranced by their greed that they forget how to escape once they've eaten their fill. The fish themselves too busy watching this spectacle to notice the net until they are bound tight in its grasp.

Us, we rarely sat in the oak table and projector room with the blindingly white paint and the steady hum of florescent tube lights. It was too cold. Too bare. Too stark. As old as we were getting, we had been flower children once. No matter the weight of responsibility and the grind of cynicism, there were those of us who still did not trust such angularity and icy certainty. We met instead in the blue. The walls were softer there. Cornflower, with windows flung wide to accept the sun. The chairs were more comfortable too, overstuffed and worn in.

I dozed in the cozy warmth of the sun while they spewed recompense and yammered about the greater good. So did most of the others. Where we once stood and screamed for the needs of others, we had become notoriously selfish in our later years. As for the money, each of us had seen greater concerns and was kept awake at night by far deeper terrors.

You ever have any pets? When you were growing up, I mean. They never mean as much when you get older, no matter how much you love them. Fitzy used to talk about this old golden retriever she had in her little years. Whenever we asked her about her dad, she'd spin another tale of Blondie. Damn original name, that. Everyone would wind up drenched in mopey bits of those last couple years. The times her eyes would suddenly glaze over or fill with rabid terror, simultaneously blank and angry. The occasions where she'd lay her head across Fitzy's lap, only to snap at her hand a second later, always licking the wound and whining after.

Those men, those women, all gleaming white wide smiles and looming black eyes, they wrapped us calmly in their knotted cloths. Slow and smooth and comforting as cocoons. Truth be told, we all missed the dancing anyways, and didn't much care what the tune was. It made us feel better when we wove in our own strains of Descartes' greater mysteries of the seat of the soul onto the dense descriptions of neural pathways and the sonic stripping away of pineal crust. It was enough for us to allow ourselves to believe.

And we craved so deeply to believe. We all had our own Blondies, our own poorly disguised metaphors. We all hoped for nothing beyond simply avoiding the curses we saw etched into the hex and rune work of twisted deoxyribonucleic ladders. That we wouldn't end up licking wounds with sad, confused gazes, wondering why the ones we love look at us that way. We didn't need much more than a gentle nudge for us to flow any direction they pointed us.

It didn't hurt anything when they mentioned the machine

would make us trip our ragged, drooping balls off.

There was a night, back in my less respectable days, when I spent the night on my back at the top of a bare hill beneath a sky, I was certain wanted to eat me alive. It was the first night I spent alone with the pretty pixie who would eventually become my wife. This methylenedioxy-methamphetamine was just medicine, a sure cure for the blues and a girl with pink weeping bandages running up the underside of her forearms. We had our worries, but not right then. Not with the breath of the earth rushing through us and our hands sliding over each other like greasy velvet and the too-far-apart stars whispering unintelligible ballads in tones only we and the bats could hear.

      So, we were all in. Foot and boot and the little pea at the center of our grey matter. Draven was the only one to ask about the inventor, Tillinghast himself. Why he hadn't been seen in decades. If he had ever actually left that old New England house to work on his device in secret, as the boardroom banter went. Or if he had simply faded away, as the trembling old ladies liked to mumble to each other over tapioca pudding and nips of cheap whiskey. Draven's eyes lit up like all hallows lanterns when he spoke of that last part.

We all knew the implications there. A flip of a switch too many and a swift goodnight to the world. Swallowed by infinity and the half-crazed music of the heart of the universe, where destruction and creation both occur so quickly that distinction between the two becomes impossible. Of course, the same people who said that also say he's become a mad god in timeless space, molecules stretched so thin as to be infinite in his own right. It goes without saying that we were too rational to fall for such obtuse nonsense, but it bears mentioning that we were also too irrationally bound up in our own fear and hope to accept the possibility.

The machine itself didn't look like much. It wasn't as bulky as its reputation would have you believe, a small thing that could fit easily on a coffee table. The lines were even smoothed out, rounded and softened. With the barely off-white color and low sheen, it looked more like half an oversized egg than anything else. This oblong hump sitting inconspicuously in the center of the room. Apparently, they had reworked the original design using more modern equipment to make it look less intimidating and more presentable for mass production and consumption.

I can't speak for the others about the treatments. Never

saw any of them after the full tests started. The yawning smiles hushed me when I asked and breathed into my ear that it was all to preserve the scientific integrity. We never met anywhere outside of that bland building anyways, so I didn't let it worry me. I can only speak to what it was like for me.

It was once a week, an hour per session. I hated the lying. I regret that as much as anything else about this. Looking my pixie in the face and telling her bold-faced untruths like that. She had to know. I was never any good at dishonesty, no matter how often and how stupidly I practiced. But a confidentiality agreement was part and parcel of the deal. Neither word nor whisper to anyone, punishable by severe legal sanctions. I didn't dare run the risk of losing out on my chance.

But the look in her eyes as I stepped out on some of those last trips, when she'd ask me again where I was going… With the sun gleaming in the wisps of golden thread that tangled outward from a head bulging with longing and on the verge of losing those giant wet drops that swelled in the corner of her eyes. Maybe it would have been better for both of us if she had simply walked away from me then and there. If she'd called me on the obvious, packed her bags and left. Then she wouldn't have been there for the tri-scaled air swimmers and great, writhing arthropods that slithered tentacles into her ears as I watched.

Now, I doubt they'd bother sending their blacked suited, jack booted, iron muscled imbeciles for me. No matter what I say. There's no point in it, anyways. The scales have fallen from mine eyes, as the man once said, but it does not a one of us any good. The cat's out of the bag and, more importantly, there's no profit in it. That, and not too many people will sit through my rambling to hear what I have to say.

I can't tell you how much I appreciate you hanging in so far. It's just not easy to keep moving forward when forward seems to twist and turn in on itself so much. Einstein melted all that illusion away years ago, when he told us that time wasn't a line as much as it was a sea and that every moment exists at once, rubbing up against each other. It's one thing to talk about, but it's another thing to see. To experience. Especially when you can't ever turn it off and ignore it. Being physiologically aware that right now I am talking to you and I am sliding flesh into flesh with that sweet girl amid the slippery dew of that hilltop. It's even worse with those things undulating and whistling around us while we talk. I tried once to plug up my ears and stop the noise, but it didn't do any good. It isn't echoing down those tubes.

I'm sorry. There I go again. I was telling you about the sessions about the new and improved Tillinghast Resonator. What it was like once that initially unnerving hum settled into your bones. Into your brain. It would be too easy to refer to it in terms of a drug. The LSD and Mescaline and Peyote we took in our gyrating youth to see past the lies and into the truth of things. Anyone espousing the similarity of the experiences is lying about one or the other.

For the first couple sessions, it resulted in nothing at all. Besides the headaches that lasted for days. Blinding bastards, they were. The kind where tiny sparkles hit your retina like the sun is dancing right on the edge of your eyelashes and the slightest sound rings like gongs hanging from your earlobes. Nothing worse than a bad migraine, wavering black spots and all, but nothing like what I'd been told to expect. In that, it wasn't too much different than most of those chemical experiences I mentioned earlier. The grating disappointment and frustration with lost time spent haggling over price points of empty Edens.

The change came slow, a creeping tide of sensation that was nearly impossible to notice at the start. More like a burgeoning clarity, as if someone had steadily over days and days, replaced your glasses with oh so slightly better prescriptions until you finally noticed you were staring at the fine hairs on the back of a fly hovering over a plate of spaghetti a half a block away. It was a sharpness in sight and sensation, to be sure, but also in the perception itself, in processing what was being perceived.

That's where the comparisons to drugs fall short. Cocaine's blinding exhilaration makes you feel like everything is in superbly tight focus, but it is only the energy coursing through you. LSD and mescaline feel like breaking barriers because they skew the experience, but they don't so much enhance it. This was something altogether different.

I knew it had to be working on my brain, honing it to as fine a point as could be had and that it would never dull. I knew beyond a shadow of a doubt that, no matter what my genetics had to say about it, no friend, lover, or stranger was going to have to scrub my feces out of a bedsheet while I mumbled about the voices in the walls. I was one hundred percent dead on certain of it and I was one hundred percent dead on wrong.

It was brilliant, in the dictionary sense of the term. The

world existed in sharper focus than I had ever seen it. I could smell which flowers were getting ready to bud by the rich, sharp tones fluttering off their leaves and which ones would be wilting within a few days by the sickly desperation of their lilt.

A woman walked by me one day, a short thing with long black hair tied up in some complicated bun over her head. I remember her almost as clearly as the texture of the grit under my fingernails. Her eyes were red and wet, bulging in sockets bordered by four pin prick freckles on each side. She was wearing a simple blue dress, something loose and airy that fit the spring weather. It was spotted in places with the telltale crusty yellow of old spit-up. She was carrying a baby swaddled in a blanket that was probably white once but hadn't been washed for a few days, so it had a dingy brownish cast. Nothing particularly amazing or interesting and certainly nothing that would be worth obsessing over under normal circumstances.

But she positively glowed with frustration and fear. That mix of uncertainty and anger that can come from nothing other than a new mother. I could see it pulsing from her, hear it screeching out of her pores, as it filled the air with a dense cloud of sweat and puke and shit that trembled against my fingertips. I breathed her in, and her terror nearly brought me to my knees. She was thinking about dropping him off at the fire station a couple towns over but knew she wouldn't because everyone in her family would have too many questions and she couldn't bare to see that pinched, judging look on her mother's face anymore.

It wasn't nearly as late-night talk show psychic as I'm making it sound. There were cues hanging on her movements, in her pheromone output, and in the way she carried herself, that told her story better than she could have if she tried on her own. It was just that I was too wrapped up in other things, too bogged down in simple sensation to notice before.

In that moment I knew, without any shadow of a doubt, that it was working. I didn't trust the wide, black pupiled eyes or the broad, stretched and toothy smiles of the white smocked creeps. All the same, no one could've convinced me to turn back then. It wasn't just the clarity of the world around me that clinched it, but the certainty inside. My thoughts felt razor edged and focused for once in my life. It didn't hurt that I wasn't spending fifteen minutes every morning trying to find my keys anymore.

She used to give me so much shit about that, especially when I woke her up at six am to help me look, shouting the whole time as if it was her fault. I'd get too pushy and bitchy. Damn near tossing the entirety of the 600 square feet and yelling my head off about being late. Then she'd look over on the bookcase and calmly remind me why we put the basket next to the door. Why the hell she didn't drop kick me at that point, I'll never know.

It took a while for things to go sideways. There wasn't any major dam breaking moment, just a slow spill and a steady leak. The proverbial frog in the boiling pot. I don't have a clue about where or when it all changed, and I stopped standing on solid ground. I just felt the air rushing past my ears one day. It's become common and mundane enough now, so long since I had any sort of firm footing, that I forget and try to act like everything is as a-okay as it ever was. It's nice to have those moments to think that I can be alright for an hour or two before I hear the roaring in my skull again.

I remember thinking that the days in the blue room, where we met for the treatments, started feeling a bit hinky. There was a frisson to the room that had never been there before. A strange tilt to the glances of the all-new staff. An off-angle reflection to the ivory in their mouths. The new carpet was hideous, like something you'd find on the floor of a mid-priced hotel. And it stank of ammonia.

For weeks, I couldn't get the acrid reek out of my sinuses. Then there was the nagging sensation of crimson among the azure, a faint reminder of meat lurking in carpet padding. I didn't really want to know and made it a point not to. By the time I started seeing them, it stopped mattering anyways.

    I feel bad for cats. They have such a horrid reputation for no good reason. Even the people who claim to like them don't get it right. They aren't nearly as aloof as they are given credit and blame for. It's more of an issue of awkwardness, insecurity, and downright terror in relation to interaction. You don't need to talk to them to pick up on it, though it helps. Just watch how they act with their own kind. Cuddling, nuzzling, and sniffing at each other within seconds, on either end, of erupting into a cyclone of fur, claws, and rage. The poor things don't know what they're doing. The basic structures and strictures of interaction evade them completely, leaving them in a near constant state of nervous paranoia. It's exhausting for the sad souls, so cut them a little slack, please.

    We were in the middle of an argument. Not with the cat. We didn't have one of those. Didn't I tell you about the dog already? I thought I told you about our dog. He was a cute one, if a bit of a bastard when it came to our expenses. Always complaining that, if we didn't spend the extra money on cable, we could afford to get him the good food he liked. The stuff made from honest to goodness animal bits and recognizable pieces of vegetables instead of the dried-up corn flour chunks that just may have once existed near a cow. No, it was with my Pixie. She was sick of me complaining that the steak tasted like Windex and rot and that this orchestra didn't play the unicorns in their Tchaikovsky like it was intended.

A shy voice somewhere in the back of my head told me that it wasn't her fault and that I should just let it go, but I couldn't. I was hooked on those twin aggravations and wouldn't give up until she saw what I saw. It was very important to me, at the time, that she understand.

I can still see it clearly. How red her face was. The tenseness in her arms. How amazing she looked, even through my own frustration and anger, in that green velvet dress. The same one she wore on our first date. They way it hugged and danced around her curves almost knocked me to the floor that night. Even in the kitchen, decades later with the two of us screaming at each other, the effect was no different. She only wore it once a year so that she could keep it in good shape.

Mid-sentence, I saw it. Barely noticeable at first, like the leftover graphite from a partially erased pencil doodle: hundreds of undulating, feathery wisps caressing her face. Some of them were laying directly against her eyes. I could see through them, to those wondrous pale green lenses but I couldn't look past them. A done bun can't be undone, as the man once said.

I didn't hear anything. The yawning mouth and wide eyes spoke nothing and let air pass without vibration or resistance. Perhaps it was just that all sound had ceased, that the atmosphere of the room had turned to amber, and all was frozen forever. Except that there was motion. Flailing. Swatting. A blur of tightly clenched, too familiar yet strangely distant hands that, against all intention, flowed through those dancing forms like smoke and landed with firm and grim purpose upon that solid form beneath. There was pain. I remember that clearly enough. Solid. Centering. Important. It was something that mattered even if I couldn't quite make out why.

Red flashed inside. The room shifted to an evil shade of orange and my arms... I was certain they must have been mine... forgot how to stop. They gave in to momentum, resisting further change. And purple that bloomed in great grotesque flowers. Unbidden, unwanted, and unimpeded upon the pale. Bleeding black coagulation into the sky.

Time wiggled in place and looped inward and forward to the hands. Not soft flitters but rough grasps of truthful, solid hands and the ragged agony of splintered bone and pulled cartilage. Somebody pressed the mute button, finally, and the sound was turned back on. They were screaming. Someone was crying in too familiar tones, an injured beast in a far-flung land screaming, squealing, and pleading. The fucking dog was still bitching about his 401k.

Somewhere deep in my self-built neural cage, I had already surrendered and crumbled to the ground. But limb and bone and sinew didn't hear. Every muscle trying its best to contract in open rebellion, even those that worked in direct opposition to each other. There was a pinch. Some insect biting me in the neck. I'm certain I saw that abomination of swirling black tendrils somewhere at the end of a restricting tunnel of light.

She visits me here sometimes. Her own dark passenger isn't always with her, but sometimes it is. She tells me about the people at work the new book she read, how she feels about the new host of Family Feud, and those strange neighbors that moved in after the Andersons went to Florida. I don't tell her about my day. I keep what I see slithering over her lips and into her mouth as she breathes to myself. The same goes with the bat that hangs from the ceiling in the middle of the day room, watching reruns of Family Guy and Married... With Children all day. I don't ask about my treatments anymore. When she asks about my day, about how I am doing, I lie. I tell her that I am fine and that everything is getting better. She smiles in that slight way that creases her forehead and dimples her left cheek, so I know she doesn't believe me. I'm certain she comes by to see me at least once a week.

  Grace, she sleeps across the hall from me. I can hear her at night sometimes talking to her husband, Ivan, about the bills and the damned Democrats and her favorite recipe for clam chowder. Telling him that he's being too hard on their son, that he should remember how much the poor boy must work to take care of his own family. Sometimes I just hear her moaning in a joyously obscene fashion. But I've never seen Ivan, even though Grace and I get taken down for our pills at the same time, and I always forget to ask in my desperation to ignore the lampreys wrapped around her spine.

I used to ask the doctors about my treatments, when they would sit me down in their offices or lay me out on those uncomfortable tables. I tried to explain what I meant when they would cock their heads and say that they were treating m/\e, but the sad and gentle tones turned harsh and demanding. It didn't matter that I'd seen it. Didn't matter that I'd felt it vibrating through my skull. It certainly didn't matter that I saw the bruise-purple, slithering, long snouted and shiny creature sifting through their papers while I talked to them. It always smiled at me when it did that.

No such Resonator, Tillinghast or otherwise, existed. Not even in the experimental phase. Something like that would be in the official journals, they told me. It would be all over the television and internet. And none of them had heard a peep about anything of its kind. Except for those times I forget, and I ramble on and lose touch with my words, I generally learned to leave it alone.

That isn't what matters anymore. Not really. Neither do the feather-flutter things or the bug-eyed, buck-toothed beasts that swim through the air like so much water or the squirrels chittering about their real estate holdings at four in the morning. Not even the hundreds of other beings that flit half-in and half-out of our dimension and others. Most of them seem friendly enough, in their own sort of way. Like neighbors who always wave hello but don't stop by to chat. What is important, what fills up the dark spots in my head, is the walls and their stark silence. The indifference of the pillows and the sheets and the chair in the corner as much as those that clean them. The echoes of nothing in the halls of the doomed and the knowledge that, while this too will some day pass, I won't even realize it when it does.

Beings in Empty: a Haibun

an absence in air,

smoke of nihil and unlight,

human shaped nothing.

Not exactly what anyone wants to be dealing with at 2 am when they needed to pee, then decided to shit, and finally realize that a glass of water after a half-bottle of Black Velvet might be a decent idea. There should be the requisite squinting and rubbing of eyes, but it isn't reasonable to expect anyone to take any of this visual input seriously enough for that. Just a bad firing of the few remaining working neurons after bathing in poison.

Dark screaming what light

will be when all energy

has been expended

But there is a point when the holes, if you can call a presence in the midst of absence a hole, of eyes bear down on you. A moment when you just have to accept that this is either a damn lucid dream, the product of one dose too many, or just reality being its usual dickish self. The time when you have to admit to yourself that you have no fucking clue what is happening. Good news is that no matter what you do, the truth of the moment doesn't give a fuck.

> And it moves one step
> One turn and a slide closer
> acknowledging you

So that you have no choice but to acknowledge it back. Look it dead in the (eyes?). Engage with whatever it has to share with you. Meet with it on its own terms. Take a second or two outside of your personal, limited view of existence. Admit that you have no remote clue in regard to this specific situation in this specific point of spacetime. A willingness to face whatever truth it may hide in the billowing folds of empty that make it up.

No dream but our loss

entropy as endeavor

No hope but our lack

And you can hear it laugh. Not so much with the standard ebb and flow of molecules in air slapping pressure on inner ear membranes as the impression of expected undulations. When those "ohs" of rounded lips and bared teeth mean joy. In the right context, devold of desire to devour, it would bear enough happiness to push aside any fear. But here, in this place? Nope. There is plenty of fear to go round.

Amygdala born

receptors bearing terror

exposed nerve endings

Where the last bit of enmity screams disbelief, and every electronic impulse says stop. When the forward motion of time and the blank face staring you down become the same. What the holy hell eats away at us all? Who sees the dreams that underpin our imagined firmament?

Smoke steps further in

a waking dream we all see

knows the truth we are

Under the Pretext of Propensity

Sweet Selena was a vision of radiance, of pure youthful sexuality as she stepped from the shower. Water cascaded gently through her deep red hair. Curving in gracefully along the back of her neck and softly over the curve of a milk white shoulder. Droplets rolled down the v of her clavicle to climb the buoyant, pert mound of her breasts. Large, but perky, defying gravity as if by the force of will. One lone bead of moisture hung from the tip of a jutting, impossibly pink nipple. More of its brethren followed the pull of gravity through the valley of her breasts down to the slight bulge of her belly, caught periodically on the light, downy hair. A bit of silver glistened in the fluorescent light: a small silver hoop in her navel. Just enough to snag attention, but not enough to scream for it. Not more than a few inches below that, incandescent pearls caught the light amid the light red fluff of her pubic hair.

"Oh...fucking...God!" Jordan exclaimed. Electricity ran

through his veins. Explosions of light erupted behind his eyes. He hadn't come with such force in years. Thick ropes of semen floated lazy circles in the toilet bowl.

A twinge of shame hit him as he looked at the image frozen on his phone's tiny screen, stopped just before she ruined it by covering herself in the nearby towel to dry off. He knew he shouldn't have surreptitiously recorded her like that. It was wrong from just about every angle he looked at it, but he couldn't help himself.

It didn't matter that she was only fifteen. Or that she was his stepdaughter. He had known her as a child, crying over skinned knees and broken dolls. Again…didn't matter. He was obsessed.

He had taken to staring when she wasn't looking. Tracing the firm bulge of her ass through tight shorts as she pulled weeds in the yard. Catching a glimpse of the creamy, speckled tops of her breasts through the unbuttoned top of her shirt as she reached across the table during dinner. Following the tight, muscular thighs as they rose to their inevitable apex between her legs as she stretched out on the couch.

Despite his shame, his horror at his own thoughts, he had to talk to someone about it before he cracked up. Maybe, if he had just kept his mouth shut, he would never have thought of using his phone on his own. Maybe he would have worked through it without going that far.

"*That's* your big problem?" Lance said, slapping his hand down on the table and laughing. At only three years older than Jordan, Lance had walked him through the confusion and terror of puberty in the way only an older brother could: by making a joke out of it at every opportunity. Still, he was the source of all sexual knowledge during those formative years and had given Jordan his first pornos. Lance had even shown him some pictures of his own ex-girlfriend *en flagrante*. Jordan couldn't think of anyone else to bring his problem to.

"Your stepdaughter's hot," Lance continued. "I don't want to speak out of turn or offend you or anything, but there it is. You've finally picked up on it."

"But what kind of creep looks at his stepdaughter that way?" Jordan said, fiddling with his glass. "Imagine what Genevieve would think of me if she knew the things that have been going on in my head. She'd leave me in a second. After kicking me in the balls a few times."

"Look, bro, women will never understand the desires that

can fucking overwhelm a man. They're biologically wired to find the most suitable mate and stick with him to make as many of the best babies they can. To hold onto him tightly as her own. That's why they freak out so much over the monogamy bullshit. Their need for stability comes from a genetic need for breeding. "But men…" Lance continued, leaning back in his chair and locking his eyes on Jordan's, "we're wired to stick our dick anywhere it fits. To spread as much seed as possible in the hope that it'll take root somewhere. Besides, a woman's reproductive viability declines faster than a man's, so it makes sense that we'd be attracted to younger ones as we get older. We can't help it."

"This isn't checking out someone's ass while we're shopping," Jordan leaned in over the table, dropping his voice lower and staring down into the amber liquid swirling in his glass. "This is her goddamn daughter."

"You've got to stop beating yourself up over this," Lance said, tossing back a quick swig of whiskey. "Sure, lust is a horrid bitch, but it's an uncontrollable one. Hell, she's not your own flesh and blood daughter. And as far as her age goes, a century ago fifteen would have been considered prime age for marrying and breeding. You can't tell thousands upon thousands of years of evolution to go fuck itself because some new-fangled societal moral compass says it's wrong. Like the man once said: 'anatomy is destiny'. We can't control our own biology."

"But…"

"But nothing. You love Genevieve, right?"

"Yeah," Jordan responded, moving the ice around in his drink with his finger.

"And damn well you should." Lance threw his arms into the air. "Bitch is hardcore. She stood by you through some serious shit and never left you hanging. And hot! No disrespect, but if you weren't married to her, I'd be begging just for a chance to hump her leg. Especially after you told me about what she did with the hot oil and ice… Damn!"

"Shit. I *am* a douchebag," Jordan said, laying his forehead against the table.

"You're missing the point," Lance said, grabbing him by the ears to look him in the eye. "You love her. She rocks every part of your world. You're not planning on leaving her or fucking around on her. Am I right?"

"Of course."

"You're just freaking out because her daughter grew tits,

and you can't keep your eyes off of 'em. I have yet to meet a pair of tits I can keep my eyes off of. As I said: you can't fight biology. It's no big deal."

"I just," Jordan said, looking over his shoulder to make sure no one else was close enough to hear, "I can't get past it, or over it. It's all I think about anymore and I'm afraid I'll do something to act on it. Make a move on her or something. I don't know how to get it out of my system."

"Damn, do you have it bad," Lance said, shaking his head and laughing. "I'll tell you what. There was this chick I used to have a huge hard on for. Just a raging pillar of bulging meat in my pants every time I saw her. I couldn't stand the sound of her voice, but her body... damn. I just couldn't get her out of my mind. I eventually realized the only option was to get her drunk enough to shut the hell up and fuck her just to get it out of my system."

"I am not going to f..." Jordan started to get up out of his chair.

"Calm down and listen, bro," Lance said as he eased Jordan back into his seat. "I'd never tell you to do that. I'm just suggesting you do the next best thing, just to work this obsession out of your head." He leaned in across the table, speaking in a quiet tone for the first time. "You take that fancy little phone of yours and you 'accidentally' leave it in the bathroom next time she takes a shower. You're always leaving your shit everywhere, so it isn't like anyone will notice. Set it to record some video and you're sure to end up with a little something to beat it to. You'll have seen everything she has to offer and it won't be a mystery to you anymore. You'll be able to move on and stop acting like such a nervous little tool."

"That's sick," Jordan responded, shaking his head and sitting up straight. "That's something a stalker or a pervert would do. That's fucked up."

"Is it? Would anyone get hurt? Would it be worse than you finally giving in one night and grabbing at her tits?" Lance was pointing his fingers in Jordan's face. "I'm not telling you what you have to, or even should, do. It's just an idea to think about."

Jordan was determined not to think about it, certain that the idea could lead to nothing remotely good. Superficially, he succeeded. However, over the next few weeks he found himself keenly aware of Selena's schedule. That she spent a good forty-five minutes primping herself in the morning had been a matter of frustration to him for several years, but he never before paid attention to the fact that she showered at almost exactly nine o'clock every night. Then she would take around an hour.

He started making a point to use the bathroom five to ten minutes before then, regardless of whether he needed to. While sitting on the toilet, instead of reading some minor bit of trashy literature, he found himself checking lines of sight. Looking for places his phone could rest without looking too conspicuous while maintaining a good view. The few times he was consciously aware of what he was doing, he excused it as a silly mental exercise. He'd never actually consider recording Selena in the shower.

Until he finally did.

Even then, he didn't dare look at the video. For two days, he repeatedly told himself that he would erase it. Never even look at it. Act like it had never happened. Treat the whole thing as a momentary bit of weakness. Several times that first day, he pulled it up and started to delete it but didn't hit the second button to confirm. Finally, he found himself in the bathroom, with no one else at home. The file pulled up. He hovered over the decision: view or delete.

It isn't like it'll actually hurt anyone, he thought as he pressed the button, blood flowing in a rush to his groin.

Selena didn't come home that night until dinner. It had been long enough for him to work out the guilt he felt over masturbating to her image. He had calmed down and felt relaxed for the first time in months. Certain that, for once, he wouldn't have to be vigilant over where his eyes drifted. Wouldn't have to force his attention on the mashed potatoes and run out to work on the car the second he finished forcing food into his mouth.

I'll be damned if Lance wasn't right.

They all sat down around the table and the conversation was trite and dull, but he was excited to be able to focus on it. Genevieve was angry at some stupid bitch at work who was angling for her position. Selena passed the geometry test she spent two weeks studying for, but barely scraped by with a C. She endured some light admonishment and smiled at the encouragement Jordan and Genevieve tried to offer. Jordan talked a bit about the customer he didn't punch, but very much wanted to. All in all, nothing special.

Then, about halfway through the meal, Selena yawned and stretched. A simple thing she had done many times that he never bothered to notice. Her arms slowly pulled behind her, in a slight inverted V and her head thrown backwards, back arched and breasts thrust into the air. Those soft, curving domes formed into perfect shape by the bra whose faint outlines could be seen through her light t-shirt.

It was quick; a moment sped through and unnoticed by the other two. They continued their conversation, but the words blurred. That single pose remained frozen in his head, overlaid with the memory of how those same breasts looked without any covering, nipples pert with freedom from the constraints of clothing.

The words had stopped. Genevieve and Selena were looking at him strangely. They must have said something to him and were waiting for a response.

Shit, he thought, *what the hell were they talking about?*

"I'm sorry," he said. "I must've spaced out for a moment. I, uh, really have to go to the bathroom."

He didn't wait for a reaction. Doing his best to surreptitiously pull his shirt to dangle over the front of his pants, hopefully concealing the raging erection he was sporting, he got up from the table and rushed to the bathroom. The second he was in there; he ripped his phone from his pocket as if it was something alive and trying desperately to attack him from its place of hiding.

The video pulled up again and he forwarded it to the single frame he needed, sitting at exactly the twenty-two minute and thirty-three second point. He was a bit surprised that he already had the exact point memorized. He pulled his pants and boxers down around his ankles and squirted a bit of lotion into his hand from one of the several dispensers on the sink.

"I know what you were doing," Selena said, giggling some, as he returned to the table. He knew she was just needling him, but he thought he saw an odd glint in her eyes. Something slightly playful and mocking. He tensed up, but hoped she didn't notice. Certainly, she couldn't really know. " Baking an emergency batch of brownies?"

He let out the breath that had stalled inside of his frozen lungs, relieved.

"Just wait until you get older, young lady," he said, waving his finger in faked outrage. "Your own gastro-intestinal perfection will wane one day, too. There's a bottle of Metamucil being made right now with your name on it."

The rest of the evening continued without major incident, but he still found himself stealing glances at her. Watching the rise and fall of her chest as she breathed. Studying the elegant curve of her neck. Her pink nub of tongue gently smoothing its way along her lips.

That night, he practically attacked Genevieve when they got into bed. The sex was energetic, excited, and passionate as any they ever had, but he wasn't with her. In his head, it was Selena's ass he was gripping onto, her luscious pink folds he was probing with his tongue, her pussy he was fucking as if the world might end at any moment.

It continued that way for weeks. He did the best that he could to control himself, to abate his roving eyes with the images stored on his phone. To quell his lust for Selena in the bed of her mother when the pictures wouldn't. The video had begun to bore him. There was too much build up time, with too little payoff. Over twenty minutes of her humming off-key to herself before a quick second or two of what he wanted.

He decided to try again.

He spent almost the entire time she was bathing pretending to read but actually trying to figure out an excuse for going into the bathroom immediately after she left. He didn't want to run the risk of Genevieve stumbling across the phone still recording. Instead, Selena made it easy for him, coming downstairs right as Genevieve had gone into the kitchen.

"You left your phone in there," Selena said. His pulse quickened and his veins went icy. Did she know? Had she looked at it? Was this the point where she started screaming at him and his whole life collapsed because of the stupid goddamn mistake of listening to his dick and his brother? "With as much time as you spend telling me to keep track of expensive things, you should try showing a little care yourself."

Her tone was light, conversational. Quiet and relaxed. He was certain that she wouldn't be this calm if she knew what it was there for.

"Thanks," he said. "I'm sure I'd be running all over the house looking for it tomorrow morning."

"You know you would."

He went upstairs, doing his best to appear calm and unrushed but needing desperately to see what he had caught. His phone was still where he had left it, perched on the corner of the soap shelf. He snatched it up, double checked the door to be sure it was locked and opened the file, somehow managing to drop his pants and underwear to the floor in the process.

For five minutes there was nothing except the empty tub.

When Selena finally entered the frame, she was wrapped in the fluffy green floor length robe that left her looking like formless mint lump of cotton. She milled about for a little bit. Brushed her teeth. Spent a few moments making faces at the mirror. Clipped her fingernails. Combed out her hair. The wait was excruciating, but he was afraid that he would miss something if he sped through too much at a time.

    Luckily, she began to fill up the tub next. As the water poured from the spigot, she slid the robe from her shoulders. That image, on its own would have been worth it all to him. Watching that mint monstrosity edge off her shoulders and fall to the ground, revealing her pale, smooth back. She was just skinny enough to show the outline of her ribs and the faint bumps of her spine, but her hips were meaty, her ass round and heart shaped.

    Then she turned around.

    The sight stunned him. Instead of the quick glimpse between frames that he was afforded before, this was a full view from the front with nothing in the way. From her full, gloriously uplifted beasts, topped with those sweet cherry-pink nipples hardened from their release, down her light, softly rounded belly to her fiery pubic hair. He practically dropped the phone. His dick was throbbing, and his balls begged for release. Still, he held off in hopes of more.

She lowered herself into the tub and grabbed the loofah, covering it with soap. After lathering it, she began scrubbing her arms, lifting each one high as she languorously rubbed the soap into her skin. Slowly, she worked the lather into and over her shoulders, around her neck. He wasn't certain, but he thought he saw her lips purse in slight moan. The loofah abandoned, she began to work the lather over her breasts, cupping them and squeezing slightly and taking extra time with the nipples. She continued to do this for a full minute before he realized what was happening.

"Holy shit, she's really…" he whispered. The realization was too much for him. He was too stunned to do anything but watch.

Her right hand had begun to slide southward, smoothly caressing her stomach on its way to her pussy while her left hand continued to knead her tits. She gyrated her hips slowly, counter to the direction her pointer and middle fingers were circling her clit. Periodically a finger or two would dive into the cleft of her cunt before returning to that wondrous pink nub. Her head was thrown back, that deep red hair spilling over the side of the tub. Eyes closed. Clearly biting her bottom lip, probably to keep from crying out. Both the gyrating and the motion of her fingers increased in tempo, and he knew she must be cumming. Her back arched, thrusting her tits into the air, hardened nipples pointing skyward as if in triumph. Hips bucked three times before settling back down into the tub, signaling that she was through.

The whole time, he hadn't so much as touched his dick, but a thick line of semen had spurted onto the floor anyways. Still, he wanted more. He rewound back through the scene, stunned that he had managed to break lucky enough to catch this, and squirted a handful of lotion into his palm. As he worked himself through his own second coming, something he was rarely capable of anymore, he imagined himself being the one to bring her to climax. *His* hands were the ones cupping her tits. *His* palms caressing those cherry nipples. *His* fingers were exploring the depths of that pink little pussy. And she wouldn't be able to restrain herself from crying out under his adoring ministrations. She would scream the name of every deity she knew into the sky as she came.

He hadn't paid as much attention as usual and left a bit of

a mess for himself to clean up. He left the video running out, not paying attention to it as he wiped his DNA off the floor and side of the sink. He had forgotten completely about it until he heard someone speaking on the recording. Selena.

Speaking his name.

He quickly stopped what he was doing and backed up the video, hoping that it wasn't what he thought it was. After all, she could not have been calm if she caught him. He would have heard Genevieve screaming if she had been told. Still, his heart was pounding as he watched Selena step from the tub and look directly into the camera.

"I know you've been watching me," she said, speaking soft and low enough that she would not be heard outside of the bathroom. "Don't worry, I wanted you to." Her hand began to wander below the view of the camera and Jordan was sure that she was touching herself while talking. "I've been trying so hard to get you to notice me. Call in sick tomorrow. Mom will be at work and we can have some time to ourselves."

He didn't know what to think. He never intended to act on his impulses toward her. Of course, that was when he was certain she wasn't interested. Now, faced with the possibility, he wasn't as sure. He loved Genevieve and she fucked like a tigress. He shouldn't have wanted anything else. But he did. He remembered his brother saying that it was all genetic coding, that he had no choice about his desires. That clinched it for him. Besides, how often would an opportunity like this present itself?

The next morning, he waited until Genevieve left to call off from work. Selena wouldn't be up for a couple hours, since it was during a break, so he took the opportunity to take an early shower. The idea of fucking Selena with her mother's smell still on him seemed wrong. It was a bit too much.

As the hot water hit him, he was already hard. He briefly considered cranking out a quick one but decided to hold his energy. He wanted to give this everything he had in him. He grabbed the soap and began to wash himself as he heard the door open.

Poking his head out from the shower curtain, he saw Selena standing in the doorway, naked except for a towel wrapped around her waist. He gulped, suddenly a bit frightened as well as excited. He expected that he would have to come to her. He had planned on going to her room and waking her with a soft kiss to the nape of her neck before moving around to the front of her, doing his best to work her into a frenzy before giving her what she wanted. She obviously had different plans.

She reached across him, letting her dangling hair brush the tip of his dick as she turned off the water. The sensation was maddening. If he didn't watch himself, he'd come right then. That wasn't the impression he wanted her to have of him.

She then took his hand and urged him out of the shower. He was shocked even more when she immediately dropped to her knees in front of him. Without delay, she wrapped her warm, red lips around the head of his cock, running the tip of her tongue along the underside of his glans as she began sliding her mouth over him. He usually preferred a bit of foreplay rather than going straight for the goods, but he didn't want to stop her.

She was taking him all the way down to the base of the shaft. No hesitation or even the slightest hint of a gag from her as she worked her head up and down. She even grabbed his ass to shove more of him into her mouth. The sensation was tremendous. He couldn't restrain himself and came in less than a minute. He expected her to pull away when the first drop of semen hit her tongue, but she didn't. She pulled him in as close as she could get, sucking down what felt like gallons of cum.

Jordan's eyes rolled back in his head. His toes were curling and familiar convulsions were running through him. His orgasm was so intense that he didn't notice the sharp nails digging into the flesh of his buttocks at first. Or her teeth.

The bite came quick and forceful. A double-sided guillotine cleaving through the meat of his dick. The pain, coming so close on the heels of such intense pleasure, didn't register correctly. He was confused and tried to pull away, but her grip on him was too strong. With muscle power far beyond that which a fifteen-year-old girl should possess, she kept him trapped against her, swallowing both the meat of his dick and the blood that was flowing from the wound.

She continued for longer than he thought could be possible. Long enough for the agony to break through his confusion. Long enough for him to start thrashing madly to force her off of him. She'd gone crazy. She saw him taping her and lost her damn mind. Now she had <u>bitten off</u> his fucking dick and goddamn <u>swallowed</u> it. The pain was white hot, blasting through his head. He lashed out in every way he could, beating his arms against her head and trying to wedge his hands between her face and his crotch but none of it succeeded.

He could feel his strength draining with his blood and let his hands fall limply at his sides. His knees gave out and he crumpled to the floor. Only then did she let go of him. As she stood up, he noticed she looked different. It definitely was not Selena towering over him now. Her skin was taut, a deep leathery tan and cut across in places with lava-red fissures that seemed to glow even under the fluorescent lamps. Those breasts that used to jut out from her chest against the rules of physics and gravity hung low and loose, stretched like pendulums dangling toward the ground. The pink buds of nipples now wizened fingers pointing hell-ward. And her face. A tight, shiny plastic mask of humanity with orange embers for eyes looking out over a broad smile lined with triangular, sharklike teeth.

Worse still was the jutting abomination between her, its, legs. Nearly the width of a toddler's arm. Roped with purple and red veins. A foot and a half long if it were an inch. With a barbed tip glistening in the yellow-green light. The damned thing wasn't even female.

He didn't have time to consider the implications of his earlier actions with this beast before it reached down and grabbed him roughly by the hair. It jerked him up into a standing position and slammed his head, face first, onto the sink. Bright agony burst through his head as his nose exploded. His thoughts were already fuzzy from the blood loss, but now he felt distant. Detached from himself.

The beast that he had thought was his stepdaughter pulled back on his hair, forcing him to look forward at his own phone leaning against the bathroom mirror. Selena's face was on it, a recording she had apparently made for this very moment.

"You piece of shit," she said in a surprisingly even tone. "What kind of perverted asshole sneaks a video of his wife's daughter in the bath? Then you try to take me up on an offer to fuck me?

"You were the one who bought me my first bike and taught me how to ride it. You spent who knows how many hours helping me make sense out of numeric gymnastics for math. You told me to always go for the nuts if a guy tried to cross any lines with me. Was all that just a way to prime me for this?

"You're a sick fuck, that's all there is to it. Luckily, you weren't the only one to teach me a few things while I was growing up. Gramma appreciated my interest in the old ways, in the lessons she learned at the feet of her own elders, almost as much as the help I provided around the house. She used to call me her little acolyte when none of you were around. Among other things, she introduced me to one of our dearest and oldest family friends.

"I'll leave you two to get better acquainted."

The screen went black and the creature's grip on his hair tightened. While he was preoccupied with Selena's rant, he didn't notice it repositioning itself behind him

The Glorious Adventure of The Premiere Size Queen of The Appalachian Trail Inside a Positively Gargantuan Cunt

Dear Backpacker International Editorial Staff,

First timer, short timer here. I never, for a moment, would have thought it would happen to me. I hoped. Don't get me wrong there. Oh, gods of above, below, and sideways, did I hope for it. I just never expected it to actually happen. I mean, who the hell expects to end up full body down to the damn calves inside the silkiest fucking pussy they've ever come across or had come across them'?

I feel like I need to back up a bit, though. Set the scene, if you will. Give a little context.

I was hiking the Appalachian trail. I can't say it was an accident either. It all came from your own magazine. Sure, I was disappointed in the rag at first. Not at all what I expected or hoped for, to be honest. Reviews of hiking gear and talks with people who spend months out on trails. In retrospect, it makes sense. I've spent so long in my specific circle of interests that the possibility didn't even consider the merest chance of beginning to think about crossing my mind of there being a different meaning of "backpacking" outside of finding some tall, buff 'n burly Xena to throw you on her back and carry you around.

I'd spent fifteen bucks, though. Which is a tad steep per copy, by the way. I know you have to pay your writers, and I appreciate articles written by actual human beings and all, but in a closed room, I am sure you would admit that's overboard. Anyway, I'd be damned if I wasn't gonna read it anyway after dropping that cash. And y'all gave me some ideas.

Of course I heard of her. Poor lady just wouldn't stop growing. All manner of scientists and doctors trying their asses off to figure out why. Pollution runoff. Steroids in the meat. Radiation. Fucking alien impregnation. Just your everyday average freak of nature situation. Whatever the hell caused it, we had an honest to goodness two and a half story tall woman out and proud in the world. Makes my forehead sweat just thinking about it now. Even if that is about all the sweating I can do anymore.

Big women always did it for me. I know, fucking cliche. Small dude like me, just on the edge of full out little person status, being into statuesque amazonian goddesses. Cliches exist for a reason, I guess. But I got this mailer once, back in the old days when places actually sent catalogs to your house. Not sure if a friend put me on a mailing list as a joke or my purchase history pointed a clear arrow at me, but this damn thing was full of the most outlandish porn you could think of in the cold pre-broadband internet days. All your usual barnyard and septic needs were represented on the cover, but it got so much weirder and intense inside. I was only twenty. An innocent babe unaware of many of my own inclinations, let alone the heights of depravity in others.

So, when I saw an ad for a video centered on one image, a woman with a man's head completely inside of her, I was struck. I laughed about it at first. Showed it to my friends. Did the whole "Isn't this weird and gross?" thing with them. But I kept going back to it. Eventually buying the video. VHS. That was how long ago this was. Wore the tape thin. Just about wore the skin on my dick clean through, too.

Fairly quickly, I was at the point where no one I could find or pay for could do the trick for me. Even when I finally found someone supple enough and willing to work with me. That wetness. That heat. That pressure. Wrapped around me.

It wasn't enough. There is only so much depth available, even with surgical alterations and medical abnormalities. At best, getting up to my chin. Whisps of wiry hair tickling my bare neck. Exciting. Intoxicating in its own way. Enough to get off, but not *enough*. Never *enough*. Not in the way I needed it to be.

Until I started hearing about her. Started seeing her on the Jerry Seinfeld and Maurice Popovitz shows. The only places a proper sideshow existed in America at the time. Now, even those are gone. Makes you weep for a lost time, ya know? Not saying that gawking at the weirdos is a good thing, but at least they weren't being swept under the carpet by people that still refuse to treat them like human beings even as they talk about how important acceptance is. Fucking hypocrite assholes.

Denise.

An unassuming name for the one who would become the center of my existence. One interview, she broke down, and they cut the feed. Not because she was crying. That shit is always ratings gold. Get you a fucking Emmy for your honesty and heartfelt portrayal and shit. No, they cut the feed because she was crying about not being able to catch a decent fuck. What is more human than that? Being horny. Being frustrated. Being absolutely crushed inside because you can't absolutely crush someone without literally crushing them. Knowing that even the most outsized freak of a pole hauler can't do shit for you.

I can attest that love is great. Love is wondrous. Love can build and destroy empires. And love can't do shit against biological necessity.

I knew I didn't have love on offer any more than a proportionate cock. Hell, mine isn't even proportionate for my own diminutive size. But I could offer all of myself, in the most literal sense.

Denise went missing from the tabloids and trash TV and there was the same fucking war going on that had been there for the past 20 years as well as a couple new ones brewing and the latest vehement anti-gay senator had been caught chaining sixteen-year-old twinks up in their basement with a pound of butter and a gimp suit. Public attention had gone elsewhere. It was clear that she wanted her own space and wanted to be left alone.

That's when I remembered your spread on the Appalachian trail. Miles on miles of dense forest and nooks hidden among towering mountains. It was naïve to think I was the one to find her place. It was stupid to act like that was the only spot like it. It was, miraculously, kinda right.

Arrogant and idiotic. Shortsighted and simpleminded. Quitting my damn job. Cutting out on my lease. Selling my meager shit that would sell and throwing the rest in a dumpster behind Meijer. Then loading up on high protein and carbohydrate meals. Mostly in bar and tubed form because that is apparently the optimal calorie delivery system. Bought that OutdoorKwest 9000 pack you gave 5 stars to and a compressed, ultralight REI Trailface sack to sleep in. Then I hit the AT at the starting point in Springer Mountain and just went north.

Took a damn piece, too. No idea where to look, so just trekking the whole damn thing. One hundred percent certain that I wouldn't find her but bound up in dreams all the same. Those dreams kept me together through both Carolinas and most of Virginia. They tightened my abs and locked my joints when I planked on the sheerest points of rock I could find. Play stiff as a board with myself, as it were. Wouldn't do any good to meet her and go all limp in my dear Denise's grasp, would it?

Was in Shenandoah that I heard her. A soft, deep moaning in the wind. Near midnight but I wanted to see Dark Hallow falls by moonlight. No mistaking that particular sound as the wind or a bear or some other numbskull nonsense. Undulating registers that moved the stone as much as the leaves. Not sure how long I pushed myself along, forcing through every bit of adrenaline left in me down that steep ass descent in the deep dark that only exists in a forest in the middle of the night.

Denise wasn't the first thing I saw. No. That was one of the others. Someone else with the same bright fucking idea as my own. Limp. Pallid grey despite what had likely been a deep sandalwood skin tone. Cock still impressively erect. A deep sense of satisfaction spread across his placid face.

Four inches doesn't sound like much. So, when I say that I saw her big toe, four inches from the middle knuckle down, pale and gleaming in the moonlight, digging into the dark Virginian soil, then you might be inclined to think that six inches isn't that much. Damn near as wide as it was long It took me aback. Those squirming piggies next to it. Grasping dirt and rock. Pulsing with moaning that had overcome the wind. Let me tell ya, son, that was a sight to behold.

That isn't getting into the arch leading up from them. The curve of ankle into calf and darkly fuzzed shin leading up the mountain. Yes, my girl's hairy. You think Gillette makes a Venus in actual goddess proportions? Besides, we're mammals, fucker. We come with hair. If that puts you off, go fuck a gecko. Personally, I had a hard time keeping myself from cumming on the spot.

My two hundred and fifty thousand lumen LED flashlight traced its way along the perfect bulge of her knee and up the impeccable meat of her thigh to the thickly furred cleft at her center. Soft, deep brown hair parting at the behest of fingers rubbing and thrusting with a gentle intensity.

Enraptured with the sight, I gasped. Held my breath as a sigh heaved down from the mountain and a loose form slid out from between the fingers, riding the moss-slicked stones down the falls. Her face was beatific. A short, pixie-ish cut gone ragged and wild around her head. Glazed eyes staring content at the sky amid jutting, angular and misused bones that pointed in strange, unnatural directions. Was I jealous of her? She and several others

I saw strewn amid the stones beneath the nethers of my dear needed Denise?

It would be a lie to say I wasn't. To say that I didn't want to be the one who realized her need and sought to fill it, alone. To say that I had not dreamed of being the only one to fill her and be the expression of her needs in base earthbound form. To leave her dreaming of me as I had dreamt of her, unknowing, for decades. I'm not an idiot.

That's the problem of being a dude, though, isn't it? You are told your whole life that you should be the one to wreck her shit like it's never been wrecked before. Don't just give her a good night. Don't just make her feel wanted or desired or fucking hot. Make her fucking cum like the world has never experienced before. Because YOUR dick is so goddamn amazing. If not, then you are just a little bitchboy in a sea of bitchboys.

Even knowing that, at the heart of it all, what I wanted was just for me. I read enough Freud to think of my own return to the womb in my cozy fantasies. If I wanted to provide for others, I could've learned how. Spent time on the proper tongue technique. Listened to the women I knew didn't want to fuck me, but bitched about the shit techniques of the dudes they did fuck. Dug beneath it for the truth of what they actually wanted. There was a reason I didn't have the time for that, and the reason was that I didn't fucking care.

Seeing these bodies lying at odd angles along the sharp edges of the stones, bent by gravity and her muscular contortions, left me feeling jealous. Angry, to an extent. Hurt by a large margin.

All the same, I wasn't quite so blinded by my own self-importance to shuffle aside my desires. I won't say that I didn't take the time to think about how these bodies, coated in my most vaunted Denise's interior lubrication, brought her more or less pleasure than my own form could. I just realized that if I played my part to the hilt, then we could both get what we wanted from this.

Not too bad of a deal, all considered.

I won't lie and overblow my confidence in the moment. Walking up on a woman more than five times your own size is intimidating. Even mid clit rub with the still twitching and occasionally cold bodies of momentary lovers cast to the waters around you. Those waters running with as much cold blood and effluence as cum. Even with all the porn and shitty magazines of my youth screaming that a moment like this is a slam dunk, my nerves stabbed me right in the gut.

Unthinking, I stepped forward. At several points, someone lay in my path. This one's breath hitching with blood-clogged lungs. The next one shitting out their own entrails in thick blue ropes. Another a mess of mangled, misplaced limbs snapped and twisted into each other. There was no need to pay them any mind. I would suffer their fates and more just to feel her interior embrace. I'd made my choice.

Near enough and her musk was overpowering. Thick. Animalistic. Oily and somehow sweet. Intoxicating. Overwhelming. Just, well...

Fuck. I'm at a bit of a loss for words to describe it adequately. Just try, if you can, to remember the first time you found yourself face deep in someone's pussy. Not all Summer's Eve hospital disinfectant reek but the real shit. Skin and sweat and day long soaked in musk with the sheen of vaginal mucus all slick and sticky on your tongue and filling your nostrils. Meaty, but not in the food way.

Fleshy.

Yup. That's the word I'm looking for. Not something to fill

you, but something to fill. Not a damn thing below the neck works on me, but I can sure as hell get my brain harder than a ten-peckered owl remembering that scent.

That's where I was. Standing between thighs pulled up toward her chest, thicker than any living tree trunks near us. Those fingers working lazy circles around a nub of flesh damn near the size of my head. Enflamed red and poking out from between her spread vulva. It was like the bright light of heavenly grace, were I to believe in such things.

Mist covered her from just below her ribs on up. That saddened me. I hoped, if I could look into her eyes so far above me, that I'd see the same kind of hunger and need I felt. I went ahead and imagined the face I saw so often on tv. Tawny and glowing like beach sand at sunset. Those soft brown eyes, pinched nose and sharp-angled chin. Thin, pink lips split with mischief just enough to reveal gleaming teeth that could well be my tombstone, and I wouldn't care in the slightest. All framed by curls and waves of hair so deeply brown as to be almost black. A starlet from Hollywood's golden age so much larger than any silver screen could fit.

It was definitely do or die time. I stepped in closer.

I began caressing the edges of her vulva. The rough texture of her pubic hair maddened me. Every primal piece of me screamed to dive into her like the deep waters of a lagoon. I knew better than that. If there was time, there would be time. I was here and there was no need to rush it.

Maybe she moaned. I want to believe that was what I heard. Not the wind blowing low through the trees and mountains, but a catch of pleasure in her lungs. Her fingers stayed their course around and over her clit. I kept my hand in rhythm with them.

Her hips rolled, edging her towards me. A slight enough movement for her, but it damn near knocked me on my ass. My face pressed for the moment against her minora. I couldn't help myself but run my tongue along that velvety flesh to taste her. I can't remember the flavor. Can you imagine that bullshit? Too overcome by the electricity pulsing through me. The excitement that wracked my body with convulsions and the pulsing of my prostate in an unexpected and positively devastating orgasm. If I have any regrets, that's where they lay.

I wonder what it felt like for her. Probably nothing. Maybe the slightest wisp of a nerve lit up, like being brushed by the leg of an ant or kissed by the wing of a butterfly.

That's when I felt a grip on my legs and hip. Probably not the entirety of her hand. Enough of it to hold me firm, though. I took the cue and stiffened myself. Remembered my breathing and locked both joint and muscle. Tightening and loosening just the right ones to keep my body rigid. Even when she had me in dead, open air, I was stone made flesh. Rigid and strong.

Now, any free diver will tell you that you think you can hold your breath until you are 200 meters down and your lungs are screaming for air but you still have that same amount back to the surface and have to ignore every natural impulse at one third of the way to open your mouth and suck in whatever is around you before the blackness takes you in. I'd followed tutorials online. Swum out into open ocean and straight down. Practiced timing myself in my fucking bathtub. Not a damn bit of that prepared me for being down past my hips in muscles that squeezed to just the point of collapse before releasing. Pulling you back out into open air for the merest second of a chance to gulp in a breath before slamming you back in. A nail of what I presume was the other hand scraping raw skin from your back at periodic, random intervals.

It was everything I'd hoped for. Everything I'd dreamt of. But so much more than I'd understood. The in-out in-in-in-in-out-in-in of it all. I remember my collar bones breaking. My knees cracking and twisting the wrong direction. My spine. Something happened. Something like the wondrous, snap-crackle-pop of existence. I was born and unborn times beyond counting. Bones kneaded. Organs rearranged. Skull meat compressed to a single searing point of incandescence. Physical, psychological, spiritual, and philosophical upheaval via pressure and release.

I heard and felt undulations undreamt of. I knew her pleasure through her flesh. I filled a need left empty by eyes that desired and despised in equal measure. I, among so many others, helped her feel human for a screaming into the uncaring sky ecstasy moment. We helped her cast aside the stares and the judgment and the assumption that existence must be in one singular manifestation.

Explosions of light and color. The dense interiority of experience occurred. I don't know what the fuck you want from me here. I wasn't, and I was. I am now and will never have been. My experience of Denise and her experience of me were. I still am. I'm not sure why. I assume someone else saw me. Did what they could to preserve flesh and neural connection to it. They wanted to help and I can't blame them for it.

How could they know the ecstasy? How can they comprehend, never having experienced, a moment wherein all later moments cease to bear importance? How could I convey to them, even with the few words that remain to me, how complete I am now?

I've begged them to stop hunting her already. I don't know what good it will do, knowing the hate held by those that can't find what they desire. What anger the weakened harbor toward those with strength they didn't ask for. But I've done my best to try to not to be another excuse of violence as a response to inadequacy and erectile dysfunction. I hope Denise is still out there and that they haven't turned her into another example of what happens when the vaginally enhanced make the mistake of acting in their own interest for once.

I hope that those who found me crushed and content did not take my lack of vocal capability as encouragement of their rage. Of support for their assault on someone who possesses what they lack. Of some resentment based on what I now lack in comparison to the experience that lead me to this state, have not pushed further against those who did not choose their present state and still refuse to find shame in it. I hope that my dearest Denise, who had the presence of mind to flee the scene where my own shattered form was found, has found her own peace somewhere in the world and is not lying, broken and rotting along some abandoned riverside. All of us forgotten and grotesque beings deserve our futures, dearest.

Anyway, I wanted to thank you for all you do. If you ever think about shutting down, please remember that there is a quadriplegic out there who would never have gotten nearly his entire body shoved into a giant's pussy repeatedly until the vast majority of his bones were crushed and nerves rendered useless were it not for the work of your fine writing staff. It has meant the world to me.

Thankfully and gratefully,
Ben Gifford

Interchangeable Parts

"A commodity appears at first sight an extremely obvious, trivial thing. But its analysis brings out that it is a very strange thing, abounding in metaphysical subtleties and theological niceties." -Karl Marx

The sensation wasn't quite like waking up. There was no long, open mouthed yawn and stretching of limb and ligament. No stiffness to be worked out. No fluttering eyelids. No eyelids to flutter. Not a single limb or ligament to stretch. No mouth. Just a burgeoning awareness of relentless revolution. Perpetual motion fed by heat without warmth. A deep, abiding cold at her core.

Everything fit precisely. Teeth interlocking without a millimeter of give between them. Screws meshing, never scraping as they turned against each other. Belts wove tight like harp strings along wheels oiled and whisper quiet. Meticulously controlled motion. A symphony of percussing presses, the soft whisper of grit polishing brass, the keening wail of steam vents and the roaring voice from deep in its belly. All so intricate, so precise, but removed from context, whirling in her lonesome corner, it made no sense.

Elsje's thoughts were fuzzy, confused. It must've been the spinning. Always spinning. Had she been spinning like this forever? She wasn't sure, but she didn't think so. Hadn't she been warm once? Felt something besides grease and grit caked along her skin? She'd been more than a formed lump of iron whirling within this dark heart of moaning metal, she was sure of it.

There had been warmth once. Light like honey pouring over her. Wind playfully pulling at the tangles in her hair. Muscles that stretched and burned with use. Skin occasionally torn in small, raised lines that oozed minute red droplets. Burrs and thorns barely noticed but an exquisite, integral part of the vast expanse of green and yellow, of the running and falling and running again. Rough explosions of air bursting out from her lungs. Laughter.

Her brothers (Hendrik and Rudolf- the names floated up from the thick sludge of her subconscious) chased her through the field because she had taken something from them, but she couldn't remember what. There was a vague impression in her mind of something small, cold and round held tightly in her hand. Something insignificant compared to the soft grass swishing against her legs, the giggles and taunts from both within and behind. Dierlijke. That's what they called her, because of the long, thin fingers her father told her were delicate, but they merely called bony. Fingers that could deftly reach into their pockets without their notice. It had been one of her favorite games; stealing little trinkets from their pockets and taunting them with her new prizes before running off, back when motion wasn't quite so stationary.

Someone had sent her here; she remembered that now as well, though she could not remember who. The warmth had become too much. It consumed everyone in her family. Not pouring over them but burning them from the inside out. Water boiled up from her own insides when she was told to be strong, like steel, like iron. To go to this new place to make a new family. Fresh off the boat, sea salt still coating the inside of her nostrils, the calls of gulls in the air and a newly processed work visa gripped tightly in her hand, the first thing she saw was Major Marjoram's Miraculous Manufactories stand. Back then, she had been entranced by metal, by the gleam and glisten of newly polished mechanical workings. Especially the gadgets and gewgaws some of the fancier men would have with them as they sauntered through town. The one with the clockwork dog stood out in her mind, all brass gears and steel springs shining bright enough to rival the sun as it clomped and clanged down the street. It was inevitable, then, that she would be drawn to this man, she was certain it was Marjoram himself, calling out to the new immigrants in a loud, boisterous voice. Other company barkers were there but lacked even a glance to spare for their bland brown cotton suits and prim demeanor. They curtly outlined their requirements and explained the terms of hire before directing men (always men, never women or families) onto overloaded horse carts, but Marjoram, in his tall, felt top hat, flashy green vest and gold buckled boots, yelled, cajoled and danced at his table.

"You, Ma'am," he called over to her, staring intently through the strangest pair of eyeglasses she had ever seen. Thick and small-lensed with leather and brass fittings and strange small parts that whirred and clicked as they moved in and out. "Come here and embrace your future at Major Marjoram's Miraculous Manufactories."

She had been very timid, confused. He must've been

talking to someone else, though there were no other women by him. She hoped to find work at a dress maker's shop since her mother had taught her to sew a bit before the flu took her, but that was as lofty as her hopes had dared fly. Why would a man of such obvious importance want a poor Dutch girl for anything?

"Yes," he continued, "you, dear." She remembered his firm grasp upon her shoulder as he pulled her to his table. "Do you know what these are?" pointing one heavily ringed finger to those bizarre glasses.

"No, sir," she replied. She did not have a particularly strong command of English, but she knew enough to fake her way through a conversation as long as the other person didn't ask too many questions.

"These are my Inward Sight Goggles, my dear lady," He tapped a gleaming brass button that set its intricate clockwork gears whirring, the lenses moving in and out while mechanical irises within contracted and expanded. "They can see deep into the very core of your being, into your soul and its most entrancing depths. They show me everything I need to know about a person, everything I need to know about *you*, my lady.

"For instance, I can see that you have an eye for detail. I

can see that those fine, delicate hands are as steady as that lady in the harbor. I can see that you take pride in what you do. I can see that you certainly did not travel over an entire ocean to work as a seamstress. I can see that the only place for you must be at Major Marjoram's Miraculous Manufactories."

She didn't notice the quill until he had pressed it into her hand. An honest-to goodness peacock feather, metallic green and black glistening in the sun with a fat dollop of indigo barely hanging onto the tip. Just holding it made her feel important, austere.

"We provide a place to lay your head," Marjoram continued. "Right near the manufactory, so you needn't worry about transport. We also start you off with an advance credit at the company store for food, clothing, or whatever else you may need. Since the balance is taken directly out of your pay, you never have to worry about paying your bill on time. We take care of it all for you."

His smile grew larger with every word. His teeth nearly blocking out everything else. Gleaming. White. Brighter than the bleached paper he was pushing towards her. The symbols and scribbles splashed across the page meant nothing to her, but she understood what it was. She'd had to sign several documents both before and after the trip.

"Would I... Could I..." she stammered, unable to find the English for what she yearned. Her hand moved toward his Inward Sight Goggles, almost of its own volition. She wanted to feel them tremble with motion and activity. To feel the soft whir and rumble of the gears. To know they were more than magic. He snatched her hand out of the air. The movement was so sudden, so forceful that she was afraid she had done or said something offensive. His grip was like iron, and he locked her eyes with his gaze, his own eyes magnified by the lenses to the point that they appeared to be gigantic pupils sucking her into their depths.

"See them?" he replied. "Touch them? Learn how they work? How they're made? My dear, you'll be the one making them. Them and many more wondrous items. You'll know them all so well, you'll swear you were part machine yourself."

The ink spilled from the quill like thick, blackened blood as she signed her name across the bottom of the paper and she swore Marjoram's smile grew even larger, sprouting more teeth than she thought possible for a person.

She first sat down in her spot on the line that same day.

Her station was bare, uncluttered. A single wooden stool in front of the conveyor belt with a small table just off to the left. She saw the machinery working beneath the belt, solid iron gears clanking and churning, grinding against one another. The thick grease coating them a dark, viscous black full of the dust and detritus of the floor, flakes of metal from their own worn brothers and bits of rubber sweated from the belt itself. Yet they continued with their work, perpetual motion without rest or end. On the table, laid out on a pristine white cloth, line upon line of three-quarter inch, highly polished brass gears, each one catching the scant light and hurling it into her eyes with enough force to practically blind her.

  A fellow Nederlander, tall and red-faced, provided her with a quick orientation and explanation of the job. It was simple: place a gear correctly into each item that came down the line past her station. They had to be placed precisely and cleanly, so she was given a pair of thin cotton gloves and a pair of needle nose pliers, with their cost defrayed to her first pay day.

  "For Christ's sake, don't touch the brass," the Nederlander told her. "You'll get your filthy prints all over it and we'll have to re-polish the whole damn thing. Then they'll take the cost out of your wages. Also, cross talk is strictly forbidden during your shift, so keep your mouth shut unless you are talking to the line supervisor. Not that it matters much, it's company policy to never place people who speak the same language near each other. Just keep your head on straight and you'll do fine."

From the start, she had been entranced by the multifaceted glimmer of highly polished brass parts. Locked together in an intricate puzzle, an ephemeral conglomeration of cogs and gears that shone as brightly as the sun. Teeth meeting and twisting. Springs spiraling in an ever-widening gyre. Screws and pins stalwartly holding it all in place, keeping it all from collapsing into chaos. So many parts, such detailed craftsmanship, so beautiful that, whatever it was, it had to be a thing of great use. And she was a part of it now, as much as she was a part of this great, expanding country. She was adding to the quality of life, making the world a better place. One small piece at a time.

"Stop staring off into goddamn space and put the fucking gear in," a harsh voice jarred her out of her revere. The line supervisor was a short man. Pudgy, with round cheeks and wiry brown hair that flailed out from his head as if it were trying to whip at everyone around him. This was the first time he had talked to her. "You goddamn hold up production any goddamn more and we'll goddamn dock your goddamn pay."

The rest of the shift went without incident. The simple, repetitive motion quickly became second nature to her. Every item was the same, the placement of the gear the same. After a couple hours, she didn't have to look to place it correctly. Motion, constant and smooth until, after twelve hours on the line; the whistle cried out a series of three short squeals, signaling the end of the shift.

Her room was in one of three long, blocky brick buildings behind the manufactory. It was small, but not much more so than the one she had slept in back… she kept thinking of it as home, even though she knew this was her home now. The walls and the floor were bare, unfinished boards, water stained in places and the beds weren't more than bare, lumpy mattresses on simple metal frames, but she didn't care at the moment. She was tired, her brain dull from the day's work. The only thing on her mind was finding which of the eight beds crammed into the room belonged to her. She had been told it would be the one in the far-right corner, but that couldn't be right. Someone else was already there. Another thin, pale girl like herself, red-haired and bleary-eyed, slowly, methodically tying her shoes. When Elsje approached, the girl looked up at her without the slightest bit of annoyance or surprise.

"Oh, I'm sorry," she said, a bit slurred and dreamy. "You must be the new one. I'll be out of your way in just a moment. I don't normally oversleep like this, but I've been running double to cover for Jeanie. She's pregnant and really needs the rest some days. Anyways, I didn't hear the whistle at first. Didn't even notice the others tramping out the door until Antonia smacked me in the head to wake me up. I promise it won't happen again. I doubt you'll even see me most days."

At that, this other nameless girl with whom Elsje would apparently be sharing a bed, drug herself up and stumbled hurriedly toward the door. Without bothering to change into her nightclothes or ask about blankets, she collapsed onto the bed and into oblivion.

From that point, it all fell into a simple cycle. Wake. Dress. Breakfast. Whistle. Walk. Sit. Pinch. Lift. Place. Breathe. Secure. Repeat. Repeat. Repeat. Repeat. Whistle. Lunch. Whistle. Sit. Pinch. Lift. Place. Breathe. Secure. Repeat. Repeat. Repeat. Repeat. Whistle. Dinner. Home. Undress. Bed. Sleep. Wake.

Dress...

So it went; the pattern unbroken, save for Saturday night's liquor-sweet revelry and Sunday's shut-down recuperation which themselves became part of the pattern. Days bleeding into weeks bleeding into months bleeding into years. Her life an echo chamber, hearing nothing but itself into eternity.

By the eleventh hour of what would be her last shift, she had settled into her usual numb, empty blur. Repetition had bred comfort, a trust in the muscle memory and automatic movement that had worked its way into her flesh, bone and tendon. She didn't need to think about it anymore and had time to let her mind wander. This was nothing new and was in fact how she spent most of her days anymore. Even if something went wrong, a previous part out of place or a hiccup in line operation, she noticed the change on some deep unconscious level enough to adjust as needed. However, she didn't take into account the toll sleep deprivation would take on her reaction time.

The night before, her turn on the bed had been cut short when the day shift returned a full three hours early. They met their quota ahead of schedule and had been sent home. Sixteen people in a cramped room that barely fit the suggested eight, half of them complaining loudly about the loss of pay and how it meant that the company store wouldn't even sell them a single bottle of whiskey on credit. It was too much for her to sleep through.

Mind and body both were dull, mushed, and she didn't immediately notice when the gears caught the hem of her dress. Everyone who worked the line knew to stand at least a foot away from the conveyor belt. This kept any articles of clothing or limbs a good foot and a half from the actual workings of the line. However, Elsje's short arms couldn't reach from there. She had heard the same stories as everyone else, even seen a girl or two lose a finger or hand to the machine over her five years on the line. Still, standing closer was the only way she could do her job. There were close calls every once and awhile. She'd lose a shoe or have to hem her dress a few inches higher, but she reacted quickly enough to leave only minimal damage and never once had to pay back more than half a day's wage for lost productivity. Each time, she said it would be the last.

    This time, it was.

Just as her mother taught her, she bought only the thickest, sturdiest cotton for her dresses. Material designed to last for years, even under harsh use. By the time she acknowledged the slow, steady pull on her dress, it had devoured too much of the material for her to simply tear free and her scissors were out of reach. The other employees around her didn't move quick enough, likely didn't understand her cries of "Snijd me los!", and her left leg had been drawn in at the knee before anyone came to her aid.

Despite the immense pressure, she didn't feel as much pain as she had expected. She didn't even scream at first. Instead, she stared. Mesmerized by the interlocking iron teeth, black and gummy with old grease, as they bit into the pale skin and red meat of her leg. There was a slight whine from the machine at the resistance of bone, but it didn't last long. Free flowing blood and scant fat helped lubricate. About the time that her knee finally gave, with a loud crunch that exploded in her ears and nerve endings and vibrated up her spine, she realized that she couldn't breathe and her lungs burned. She *had* been screaming but couldn't hear herself over the wails of the steam whistles and the thumping of the presses. She couldn't tear her eyes from the pulped meat that oozed along gears and pistons, slopped onto belts and shot from spinning wheels. Inch by inch, the dividing line between flesh and machine disappeared before her eyes as the color faded from the world.

    The machine never stopped running and a replacement was on the line within ten minutes.

Self-Fulfilling Prophecies Always Reveal Themselves in the Shittiest of Bars

"Transcribed statement of confession from Ezra P. Nelson, courtesy of the Portland Community Police Department."

Red.

Look. You said you wanted it all. From the beginning. That's what I'm giving you. So don't roll your eyes like that. That's what I saw. Red. Flowing over everything. Waves, like tsunamis, washing over Jamie's Rose. Nathan and Yodiel, throwing those stupid plastic darts at the machine in the corner, were up to their necks in it and still smiling like the idiots they were. Leese, three empty glasses hooked into her arm and four full ones splayed in her hands for some goat-grin gaping shitbags she was serving, seemed to notice it slipping up over her nostrils. I'm pretty sure her eyes rolled back as she sucked it in. The Urban Cowboy type that filled the room with his artificial bourbon and leather cologne at full on war with the all too real unwashed pit reek cornering Anneliese with his wide eyes and flailing hands dripped it when he walked in. It was up past the eyeballs of that short, simple fuck before he started cheering, loud and full of his own self-righteousness, the recent win.

Sure. It was Carl. You need the name, right? You need to keep your fucking records all clean and crisp. Carl Fucking Tuckerson.

You want a quote? Straight damn shit from the donkey's mouth? I got you.

"Those cunts can't take our balls from us anymore!" That work for you? Yes, that is what he said. Right on the other side of the bar from me. After eye fucking my tits the whole time, he gave his order for a well shot that didn't taste like shit. Then winked at me like he did me some fucking favor. Like I was oozing from the raw, quivering fat jelly of his intense inch and a half at full mast manhood.

And the red, bright as full out Juggalo Faygo Redpop, burst through the door. Foaming. Rolling in waves that crested and ebbed over me and everyone in the Rose.

I don't do coke. Not anymore. Not after that incident with Jessie and the aloe plant. Took too long to heal from that. But the sense of power, of certainty, was damn near the same. I knew I was right. Knew I was righteous.

To be honest, I still stand by that in regard to Carl. Back in middle school, the motherfucker regularly *accidentally* wandered into the girls' restroom and hid out in a stall to try to catch some bare snatch. I'd heard him say as much in the locker room before gym class. Before... well, just before.

Lucky for Charlene and Jolene and Edna, things were a bit looser when they didn't know better. I've poured more than my share of heavy pours for those three on a late Wednesday. Choked back everything they told me about that shitbag and the gleam in his eyes as he threw a few Benjamins at them to do what they could to cover up *their* sins. Lucky that they only had to drive across the county line to scrape and suck out any remnant of his DNA before it had enough time to take root within their flesh.

Not so lucky for Shanese. Too small to trust that NO meant anything. At fifteen, too young to trust her ability to fight back. Too tired from spiked drinks to run away. Too many generations removed from knowing the right herbs to imbibe and too many miles away from a state that didn't require consent from a parent who would rather beat her to death for ruining the family name than scribble a simple signature. Shanese unwound an old wire hanger and did her best to follow the directions on a Reddit thread but scraped something the wrong way. She'd been dropping angry red-black clots and dribbling pus for a week before getting up the courage to ask to go to the hospital. Do you have any idea how many public hospitals are catholic? Ever try to find one that isn't? The ER doc said he didn't feel right treating someone who had committed such a sin before making confession. Like he kept a priest in his back fucking pocket. She never regained consciousness.

So, yeah. I saw the next wave of that crimson tide flow in. I saw it swallow good old Carl up. I saw him smile, so smug and certain of his own invulnerability, in the face of it. I actually saw that piece of shit wink at me as he cupped a hand on some random ass cheek.

That's when I sucked in the red. Closed my mouth and opened my nostrils. Let it fill my lungs like the smoke from a cracker vacation yogi's hookah. Let it envelope and invade me.

It was...

Okay. Picture seeing every neuron flip on at once. The

bright electrical light of it. A cool blue glow vibrating every part of you. Telling muscles to gogogogogo. And they do. Acting on their own. Fluid. Perfect.

One hand landed firmly on the back of Carl's neck. My left? Yeah. I am pretty sure it was my left hand. His boring ass brown cow's eyes opened wide at the touch. His thin, pale pink lips curled up in either a smile or a smirk. I doubt he knew the difference, either. I could see his lizard brain doing the math and coming up with the wrong result from the entirely wrong equation.

I pushed. Elbow somehow already looped underneath his so that the back of his gross ass black crusted nails brushed my cheek. His legs gave out. His cheek sliding on the spit and spill coating of the paneling that pretended to be hard wood flooring. Apparently, I'd grabbed a bottle with my right. Bright green, so it had to be Little Kings. I didn't even know anyone still sold those.

A quick snap of the elbow and wrist, slamming the bottle against one of the overturned chairs. It took more effort than usual because those bottles are so goddamn short. The crack and tinkle of breaking glass really is something, isn't it?

By then, he'd started whimpering. Not really fighting back against me. A passive lump of clay under my admittedly not inconsiderable weight.

Look. We all want to be dainty. With those light, gentle curves. Some of us are just built with a bit more heft and I am not about to start hating myself just because some dudes can't handle me being on top.

So, he's there underneath me, whining about something. I couldn't really tell. It was high pitched and hurt my ears. Probably sliding his tongue across a floor that likely hadn't seen a mop since before the Duke died. My hands were full, so I lifted one of my legs and hooked a few toes into the waist of his pants. Useless skill number fifty-two of ol' monkeyfeet finally proving itself not so useless. Kicking them down and mostly off him didn't take nearly the amount of work I expected. Apparently, those loose-fit, anti-constriction jeans (guaran-fucking-teed to not cut down on your sperm count, according to his earlier rant) had a benefit he wasn't expecting.

He moaned. Full out porn level "uuuhhhhhhhh." Maybe this all fit into some fantasy he had. A woman so overcome with his manliness that she just HAD to tear his clothes off. Probably assumed I was going to start screaming for is cock inside me at any moment.

Admittedly, I did reach down between his legs. Honestly, I respect how well-groomed his ass and ball sack were. Not many guys his age bother doing anything to keep those areas in order. Who knows, maybe he had some special design or message intricately shaved into the pubes over his dick. Though I guess you all would know that by now. The pictures probably show it. And I assume it would be a tad outside general procedure to ask to see them, eh?

Scrotums are tougher than we give them credit for. The skin is thin and stretchy, so it's easy to assume that it's weak. Could also be that the bottle didn't break as sharp as I'd hoped. Either way, there was pushing and twisting. Plenty of screaming from him and from other people around us. A bit more blood than I expected. He finally started kicking back against me. Fighters are always so much more fun, don't you think?

I guess he was right about us cunts after all.

What They Don't Tell You About the Mummy's Curse

Dear Archaeologist's Digest,

I never thought it would happen to me, but there I was. Down to the root in a desiccated throat while cracked-skin fingers rammed triple knuckle deep up my corn mine. A dream cum true for a humble soul like myself.

Let's back up. It's worth giving you time to grab the lotion or water-soluble lube and slick that fist or Mr. Fister. I get where many of you need that slippery-slick smooth motion. Personally, I crave the friction of dry scrapes. I desperately want to feel skin slough off in rough trade against unforgiving leathery dryness. You do you and I will do me.

I'll admit that I am not an archaeologist. Never had the money for school. Did have the love though. I always dug old shit. History and stuff. Wanted to know where I came from and the like. So, yeah, couldn't get the degree, but our local museum needed people with strong backs. I spent my youth tossing hay bales and picking stones. I knew how to bend and I knew how to lift and I didn't tire so easily.

Some of y'all talk shit on country boys but let me tell ya: a job needs done, we do it. Won't stop til it's done right, neither. Say what you want from your concrete towers 'til you need a bit of spit 'n polish on something, then we'll talk.

So, they hired me to unload crates. Move boxes from point A to point B. Always talked down to me like I couldn't read a damn floor plan, too. Not a one of 'em knew how to work a pallet jack, but I was the idiot.

Sure. Whatever. I got to see all o' them bits o' history. Not just the shit y'all get to see, neither. All the boring stuff ain't no one wanna take a look at. You got any idea how many ancient relics I've rubbed my rock-hard cock against? No, you don't. And you don't wanna. That's not mentioning all of the time smoothed ornaments I've rubbed up on my gooch. More 'n a few gems been dipped deep inside my ass. Several you seen on display, too. Maybe dulled a bit from whatever scraped off onto 'em, but that is just between us girls, right?

What matters is this: Big ass case came off a truck. Late at night, too. So, I was the only one there. Driver didn't even step over to piss or nothin'. Just backed up to the dock, then high-tailed it the second I unloaded the one damn crate we had. I assumed he had other pickups, since the truck was empty after I got my piece.

Now, don't you go lookin' at me weird for openin' it. Needed to know where it needed to go. 'Sides, it was just a regular box. Plain boards. No special markings. No stamps sayin' *Handle With Care: Old Dead Egyptian Fucker*. So, I popped it open, like I would anything else.

Musta jarred it enough to pop the top just a bit. The sarcophagus. Maybe he was already ready to go. Trust me, that particular Staff of Rah was enough to move its fair share of wood. Opened just enough that wafts of cinnamon and anise filled my nose. Cumin, too. I can cook like a motherfucker, so I know my spices. But my stomach wasn't the thing stirrin' in me. That undercurrent of aged meat, thick and rich. A little sweet. Popped my cock up like a steel pole.

Okay. So every movie in the history of ever should have prepped me to run when the slow, low creak of the lid moving started. There's possession, bugs under the skin, strangulation, curses, all of the like in line for those situations. But I was curious.

I wanted to see. Fuck that. I wanted to feel.

That leathery, wrinkled hand that reached out from the deep black inside. Fuck, did I want to run my tongue along the grooves and ridges of ages. Every part of me wanted to taste skin that had been cured by sand older than anything I could reasonably conceive of. Was the sun even the same sun when he walked under it?

Stuck in those damn dumbass meandering thoughts, I missed seeing him rise up, whole, from the sarcophagus. I looked up and there he was, reduced by time to the leanest flesh possible. Ropy muscle and tight tendon. Ridged. Bulging. His joints poking out at sharp angles. All of him, naked and beckoning.

Though none as much as the fuckin hog jutting out from his hips. Look. I'm no size queen. Nine inches is usually my max. But I have to admit that there was something to this beast rising from a dense bush of pubic hair. Like the fuckin four pack tube of tennis balls I get for my pitty just aimin' straight for my face.

Before I knew it, his fingers were laced into my hair. Fucker was stronger than there was any reason to expect. No way to fight back against that pull. Of course, there was no fuckin way I was going to do that, noways. I've rimmed dudes behind the dollar store for a pack of Salems and a smile. No way in hell I was gonna miss the chance to suck cock across centuries.

Sure, it was dry. Dry as West Texas wind in August. The second my lips touched the folded edges of his foreskin, ready to pull it back to get to that sweet, sensitive skin beneath, they stuck. Every bit of moisture pulled out of them.

But I'd been drooling from the moment I smelled him. My mouth overflowing with fluid. My tongue did what it needed to. Slid out between teeth. Edged itself along the inside of my lips. Nudging the raw, cracked, and leathery skin of his cock head. Like an old boot that had seen serious work in the angry sun. Dirt. Dust. Dry, dead skin flaked off into my mouth. And I sucked down every morsel.

I had to stretch my jaw just to fit his head past my teeth. He was pulling my head in closer. Thrusting into my mouth. Trying to fuck my face like I'd never worked a dick before. I wrapped my right hand around his shaft and started pumping. Yeah. My hand was dry, too. He was the one who didn't give me a chance to spit on it. Don't judge me.

I cupped the wrinkled flaps of ball skin in my left hand. Undulated my fingers to move his balls around in there like those old dingle dangle Chinese balls. All the while working my middle finger along his taint and up to his asshole.

It didn't give and I didn't have any lube, so I just pushed on through. Hell, I was pretty sure he woulda shoved his giant cock all the way through my skull if I hadn't taken control. Skin split. Cracked open. Parted for my finger. It scraped and pulled itself through. In and out. Dragging pieces of him along with it. Given the moans and mutterings he spilled in whatever fuckin language he spoke, I'm pretty sure he didn't mind.

Didn't take long, but don't you start talkin' shit over that. YOU go ahead and wait a few thousand years between nuts and tell me how long you hold out. I could feel the muscles in his ass clench 'round my finger. His balls pulling up in my hand. His cock pulsing against my tongue and lips.

I didn't know what to expect. A puff of dust to choke on? Lame, angry and bitter old semen drooling like oil onto my tongue? A single, oversized sperm wriggling its way through an overstretched cockhole before squirming down my throat?

Ended up being a pretty standard hot load. A bit saltier than I prefer. Dude could've used some more fruit in his diet. Can't really think of any fruit that grows in the desert of Egypt though.

Dates? Indian Jones had Dates. Fucker coulda eaten some dates. I ain't no bitch though. Sucked down every damn drop.

His fingers loosened their grip on my scalp. Cock wilted in my mouth. Floppy, cracked skin deflating in my hand. Motherfucker tried to back away. Like this shit was over now that he had his.

Look. Pharaoh. King. God. Street rat. I don't give a fuck. You don't nut in someone's mouth, then just wander off.

Reciprocation, my man.

So, yeah. I stood the fuck up. Grabbed Imhotep by his shoulders and pulled him back toward me. Looked that ancient son of a bitch in the eyes and made sure he saw what was up. Made sure he knew he wasn't the only one gonna get their nut that night.

A quick glance down, my eyes tracing the direction for him, was all it took. He went down on his knees in front of me. His breath hot against my stomach. My heart tried its best to pound its way out of my chest. It finally hit home. I sucked a mummy's cock. Slurped down its cum. Now, it was gonna taste mine.

I'm sure someone is reading this, getting all red in the face and triggered over the "desecration of ancient artifacts" or some bullshit. I respect history. I respect the shit in museums. Their unique, important place in our understanding of who and what we are. How fucking fragile they are. How a wrong scrape or brush of air can completely destroy them.

But, when you got yer hard cock pressed up against a pair o' dust-dry lips, ready to slurp it into the soft palate of ages, thoughts like that tend to float to the background. You go ahead and respect history with your mind and your morals. I respected the fuck outta history with my dick.

His lips were cracked. Much worse than the wasted, ashy lipped shitface in an Atlanta alley back in '18. His teeth, too. Broken and sharp. Like fangs raking along the ridged skin of my cockhead. Tongue was like sandpaper. Not cat tongue sandpaper, but *sandpaper* sandpaper. High grit tore at my skin and every nerve was on fire.

Clearly, manicures weren't a thing back in his day. Nails were ragged as fuck. Wrinkled and crusty as they forced themselves into my ass. Agony bloomed like a fuckin orchestra. Do orchestras bloom? I don't fuckin' know. Do I sound like the kinda person goes to the Met? Fuck you.

There was a lot going on. Ecstasy, too. Nerves screaming

back and forth. Confused. Overwhelmed. Even the memories are jumbled. Dice shaken up in a cup.

I didn't last long, neither. Shot my jizz down the throat of long history before you could count to ten. My brain, my heart, my soul lit up like the fourth of fuckin' July. Explosions and neon electricity. I thought, for a moment there, that I saw into the center of the sun. Definitely felt my heart turn lighter 'n a feather. Even if it was just for that second, damn did that second feel fucking amazing.

Would you believe that asshole just got up and walked away?

Yup. Just wandered off, naked as anything. Maybe he had an ancient love to find. Maybe there were old grudges that needed answerin'. Maybe he just wanted some better ass than this wasted piece of shit.

I just know I'll never find a dick like that again and the scars on my cock are all I'll have to remember him by.

Violence Works in Mysterious Ways

Celestin's fingers twitched slightly as they pinched the pale pink, delicate sliver of flesh. A subtle movement, slight enough that the assembled family and parishioners did not notice it. Perhaps Father Bernard would have picked up on it, with those piercing jet-black eyes he always kept so keenly locked on Celestin. Fortunately, the revered Father was needed elsewhere today. A home communion service for some poor, lonely widow bound to her bed with the bare remains of her life leaking slowly out through her pores. The living, no matter how close they may be to ceasing this plane, always had to come first. The thought of the Father's annoyance at this brought even more joy to the occasion.

He steadied his hand, concentrating on his breathing and heart rate. Each breath drawn bore the heady, cloying density of incense, catching and clawing at his lungs, but he latched onto it. Focusing on the interplay of smoke-borne musk and sour sweat over the burgeoning semi-sweetness of new rot helped him to block out the voices murmuring around him. The same stale nonsense they always did. Only stray words slipped through, the different voices blurring into one.

"How..."

"...never..."

"...soul."

It was always like this for him. The anticipation of that first bite. The certainty and the terror and the dread. Above all else, the hope of something transcendent. Something more than the bland mundanity of Greed and Lust slithering down his throat. Something more than the pallid light of naked bodies and the dull friction of sliding against and into one another and the stale dust of old bills filling and clogging his lungs. Something real, for once.

The need overcame him and he slipped the meat into his mouth, letting it rest on his tongue. Nothing would happen until he chewed it, until he swallowed. Still, it was a part of the ritual. The waiting and the anticipation were as integral to the experience as the consumption itself. A slight tingling, nearly electric, vibrated against the small bundles of nerves that filled his taste buds. As he slowly closed his teeth down on it, one last word slipped in past his defenses.

"...sacrifice."

A scream, high pitched and piercing, cut through the mumbles of background noise. The room washed over crimson. He felt a weight in his hand that hadn't been there a moment before. His fingers were wrapped tight around something. Muscles along his arm tensed and relaxed in concert with those in his shoulder and back. Tendons stretched with tension, pulling and being pulled. Impact shuddered through bone. Something crunched. Something shattered. Something hard and solid gave way to softness.

Bitch.

The word burst unbidden in his head. Not his thoughts, but there, among the chemical signals of his own neurons, nonetheless. Right alongside the rage. Pure, unmitigated and unstoppable. It spread like fire through his veins and soaked into the fibers of his muscles, filling them with their own life, their own action.

Cunt!

He wasn't where he should have been. Not anymore. The room was dark. Those idiotic, damnable voices were gone.

Between his toes, he felt the soft, plush fibers of a rich shag carpet. On the floor in front of him, someone had splayed out a bleached blonde wig wrapped around the splattered remains of a watermelon.

Who let Gallagher in here?

He could feel the giggles rise up and out of his throat, but hadn't felt like laughing. The juice was far too red, the pieces too grey and white. Too sharp. Too soft.

Something was twitching beneath him. A jerk-twist-jerk dance of small, declining motion. Something a piece of him swore used to twitch in that same manner for wholly different reasons. Something that promised pleasure and delivered destruction. Something that thought it was owed more just because of jellybean sized growth in its abdomen. Something that thought it could take everything everything EVERYTHING he had spent fifty years building because it was the "right thing" to do.

Rage wrapped him in its choking crimson cloak and the marble bust of Shakespeare came crashing down again, this time into her chest. And again. And again. The repetitive motion calming, bleeding out his anger to an almost zen-like sense of comfort. Shards and splinters of rib punctured the skin around the cavity forming in the center of her chest. A single plump plastic bag slipped free from the flesh on the left and settled into the bowl of raw organ and tissue.

"N-n-n-never would admit those t-t-titties were fake." The voice coming from his mouth was alien. Manic and catching on itself. He didn't stutter. He knew that. He also never let his nails grow as long as the gnarled, unkempt growths he saw stretched out from the ends of equally gnarled fingers.

Fingers that released the reddened marble bust and moved to the empty space of its chest. Marla, dammit, a quiet voice screamed from somewhere distant in his head. Her name was Marla. Of their own accord, those fingers reached into the void that had been Marla's (Its) chest and grabbed onto the shredded skin of the lower half of the wound. His knuckles went white with exertion. Muscles in both his upper and forearms shuddered with the stress he/not-he was putting on them.

He expected something similar to the sound of ripping denim when the skin finally lost cohesion. Instead, it was far wetter, significantly softer sound. Almost a sigh of parting flesh that reminded him of their first night together. Just like that night, the fingers did their work, digging in as deeply as they could.

Grabbing. Pulling. Tearing tissue loose from ligament until a limp piece of translucent flesh, roughly the size of a jellybean, lay cradled in the palm of his hand.

"G-guh-gummi B-b-earby." Laughter shook him and he couldn't be certain of the source. Between his teeth, bones he did not expect crunched in a satisfying manner.

From there, the experience became a blur of promises made and money passed between palms. Midnight arguments. Tears born more from fear than sorrow. Reassurances. Acceptance. An absence that slowly slid aside, giving way to the soft rumbling of inane conversation, poorly varnished wood panel flooring and the mercurial tang of salmon on his tongue. Celestin blinked three times, slowly.

He was back in the room he had never really left. The parlor of the funeral home. Edward... Scratch that. Doctor Edward Liston Jenkins. The esteemed and grieving Mrs. Doctor Jenkins made it abundantly clear that he was not to be referred to as anything less. *He had not spent a decade and the better part of his inheritance at Oxford to be called anything as vulgar as his first name.* Doctor Edward Liston Jenkins lay on the table in front of him. Pallid and motionless as any decent corpse should be.

Unbound by clothing, lumps of fat rolled over the side of the slim table, their undersides purpling from the blood that had begun to pool there.

Several other slices of raw salmon, the good Doctor's favorite food according to his wife, lay on various key junctures of his body: his forehead, just to the left of the center of his chest, the tanged gray bramble of his pubic hair and in his left hand. Each morsel set to draw out a sin tied to that particular area of the body. A particular sin that Celestin would take on as his own through consumption.

Each man's sin is his own, Father Bernard's voice echoed like rain on stone in Celestin's head. An inflexible, sanctimonious fool who never approved of his kind or his work. Always scowling and lecturing, even as he counted the money desperate family like the good Mrs. Doctor Jenkins gave to the church. *It's his burden to bear and his to atone for. Or not, should he choose so.*

He picked up a thin slice of salmon from the other hand and placed it in his mouth, knowing full well he'd already experienced the best Eddie had to offer

***

"So, she knew about it," Finn laughed around white, greasy

noodles that hung from his mouth before slurping them in. Celestin hoped reducing the lighting of his sparsely appointed cell to bare candles would save him the sight, but the glare of the tiny flames seemed to search out every spray of spittle. "Even the cleanup?"

Finn's table manners, or lack thereof, disgusted Celestin. Regardless of who they were and what they did, there were certain lines of acceptable behavior. However, he couldn't afford to be overly picky about whose company he kept. In their line of work, neither of them could. So he humored Finn with the lurid details he always asked for once a job was completed.

"Knew about it?" Celestin carefully chewed his own moderate forkful of linguini before continuing, relishing the sting of the garlic and the sweet overtones of basil. "Half of it was her plan. The half that actually worked."

He slapped the table to punctuate the joke, even though he didn't feel the enthusiasm he was showing. The rush of the moment, the excitement of the shared experience wasn't what it used to be. Anymore, it left him feeling flat. Empty. All the same, he couldn't imagine slinking home and slumping into the lounger, lacking even the energy to turn on the lights or the TV. Therein lay the first step down a steep, muddy path that ended with the taste of oiled metal in his mouth and the flash-bang of pressurized gunpowder. So he would humor Finn. Give the man what he wanted, so long as he stayed in the room with him and kept the silence, the void, at bay for a little while longer.

"It's guaranteed return business, then. Did the dear old Missus Doctor go ahead and lay out the retainer fee?" Finn rubbed his pointer and middle fingers against his thumb in the universal sign and grinned.

"No such luck there," Celestin let his head drop a bit, unable to hold up the act for the moment. "The look she gave me... even when she was shaking my hand and thanking me. You know the one."

"Sure." Finn placed one Alfredo-slimy hand over Celestin's. "The 'please, God, stop touching me before something rubs off on me' glare. Fuck that bitch. She'll be back sooner rather than later. The next time some asshole comes too close to running her down in the street and she'll beat down your door, begging for the healing touch of the martyr."

Celestin felt Finn squeeze his hand slightly. He knew he was supposed to look up, that this was one of those 'connecting moments' where reciprocity was expected. So he raised his eyes and fought back the inexorable pull of gravity on his eyelids. Just as he expected, Finn's dull brown eyes were locked on his.

"Then you charge her double!" He burst out into laughter, his face beet-purple and eyes bulging with the force of it. Pieces of half-chewed noodle flew from his gaping maw. Celestin knew he would have to scrub down the walls later, but the sight was too absurd to keep his composure. He allowed the giggles to ripple up from his diaphragm. It didn't chase away the empty pit inside of him, but it at least felt like something real.

"I know that isn't the issue," Finn said, after catching his breath. "Not the real one anyways. We both've been doing this too long to let some prude's upturned nose have any effect on us." He stood up from the table, arms thrown wide and head cocked at an extreme angle against his shoulder. "We're the ones that bear the weight of their crimes. The ones who carry hell on our backs so that they can sleep easy in the knowledge that their loved ones have moved on to an unearned reward in heaven."

"Yeah," Celestin muttered, waving his hand dismissively, "right."

Such blasphemy in the eyes of our one true savior, Father

Bernard's cold admonitions against such easy forgiveness still clawed at his psyche. *An arrogant mockery of the miracle wrought by blood and flesh.*

"Just because it is a myth," Finn chuckled, "doesn't mean we shouldn't let them hold onto it. Let them keep looking at us as the saints they love to hate. So pure and selfless that we would be willing to take their time in the flames as our own." He leaned in, nostrils and eyes wide as he spoke. "As long as they keep bringing their deep, dark unmentionables to us, what do we care?"

"That's the thing," Celestin said into his empty bowl. "They aren't that deep or dark or unmentionable anymore. Just the same mundane nonsense. The flashes of red rage, the splashes of blood and the memories of someone else's hands rending meat and muscle just don't do anything for me anymore. The moment itself is fine enough, but it fades into the background too easily. Disappears too quickly."

Fin sat back down, landing in his seat a touch too hard. The cheap wood groaned under the extra pressure. The laughter left his face. His grin settled into a thin, pursed line.

"I know what you mean." He let the words slip from between his teeth. "What was the line from Conan? Something about the time coming when rubies cease to sparkle and gold loses its luster..."

"And all a man has left," Celestin added, barely whispering the words into being, "is the aching desire to know what it feels like to grip a living man's throat between your teeth and clamp down. To know that the memory and the act belong to you and you alone."

"To earn your own trip to hell for once."

Finn turned away from Celestin with that last statement. The silhouette of his mouth against the fire opened, then closed again. Celestin heard him draw in a deep, slow breath. Then it came pouring out.

"Look," Finn said, "I wasn't going to tell you about this. I'm a fucking moron for even considering it."

Another deep inhalation. This time he remained silent after expelling it.

"What," Celestin asked, "are you talking about? This isn't the first time either of us have bitched about this particular problem. Hell, you were the one who brought it up the first time."

"Yeah, but this time," Finn paused, index finger resting against his temple, "I may know of an opportunity. A way to address the issue with little to no personal risk. Something I picked up from my last job. The lawyer.

"So much of what I took from her tasted like ash and held as much substance," he continued. "Mostly altering and removing paperwork. Forged signatures allowing the movement of funds between accounts that weren't officially sanctioned. But, between bouts of pension theft for greedy trust fund brats, there was something regarding communication of a fluid location. A man that offered certain experiences. For a pretty penny, of course. She took the money and gave the location, a buffer between the client and the," Finn coughed, dramatically, "service provider."

"What good does that do us?" Celestin asked. "It's not like we can reach her for the info. Even if we could, the church watches our accounts pretty closely. You know damn well one of us could do much more damage than a few baby buggering priests."

"That's the thing I should know better than to tell you," Finn said. "She had just set up a series of clients the night she died. I know where he will be, but only until tomorrow."

***

The house wasn't what Celestin expected. Crammed in

among a cookie cutter development. Every lawn perfectly manicured with every blade of blue fescue trimmed to a uniform height. Cream and egg yolk yellow must have been in fashion when this one was built, since each house alternated between the two. Not even a differing garden or bush to distinguish any of the houses by more than their number.

He was certain Finn had it wrong. Either that or the bastard was playing a joke on him. At the same time, he knew that this would be his only chance. He also knew that, if he walked away from this now, he would end up taking the Hemingway methodology of dealing with his disappointment.

So he walked up the steps to the house and knocked on the door, noting the lack of a doorbell. A faint shuffle-shuffle-thump came down the hall, presumably toward the front.

Great, now I'm bugging someone's gramma, he thought. *Right on time to interrupt Wheel of Fortune, too.*

When it swung open before him, he wasn't surprised to see a white haired, stooped shouldered old woman hunched over an aluminum walker. One of the neon green tennis balls had fallen off the tip of the front leg. Out of habit, he bent over and replaced it.

"Thank you, dearie," she said. Even her voice shook with the palsy that had obviously overrun her. Celestin was now beyond any possible doubt that he was in the wrong place. This tired little old lady couldn't watch over a cat, let alone... "You must be here to see Jeffrey."

She turned away before he could respond and began a slow slump down the hall. Something caught his eye from under her floor length skirt. A glint of reflected light, silvery and sharp, as if from smooth metal. The same thumping he heard when he was outside occurred again, but her walker never left contact with the floor.

"He didn't tell us to expect anyone today," she continued, "but his friends so rarely bother to call ahead."

The hall went straight to a shared kitchen/dining room. On the table, a Scrabble board was set out. The empty spot at the table only had six tiles laid out in the holder. The man seated across it looked at them expectantly through yellow, watery eyes. The few stray patches of hair that remained on his liver-spotted pate grew wild and scraggly. He wriggled in his seat.

"I'm sorry to interrupt your..." Celestin trailed off, noticing that the thick black stripe across the old man's sweater was not decoration. He was clearly being restrained. Looking back to the Scrabble game, he saw that the woman, or whoever sat in this spot at the table, had already spelled out not one, but two words:

HELP US.

His stomach lurched.

"Oh, it's no bother, dearie," she cut in. "We live to make our little Jeffery happy."

She turned a corner and opened the door there along the wall. One hand reached out, pointing down the rubber covered wooden stairs into the brightly lit basement. Then she scooted sideways.

"I'm sure you'll understand if I don't show you the rest of the way, dearie," she said. Her wide, bloodshot eyes carried thick, bruise-black bags underneath them. He'd been too wrapped up in his own thoughts, his own insecurities, to notice what should have been unmistakable panic in her face when she answered the door.

Now, he was all too aware of it.

What have I gotten myself into? he thought, increasingly certain that this whole thing was a dream and that he was really lying comfortably in his bed, waiting to wake up with a horrendous hangover.

You've gotten yourself into exactly what you wanted, douchebag, chimed in a warring voice in his head, disconcertingly similar to Finn's. *You wanted something real. Something personal and concrete. So stop whining and suck it up. What the hell do you think someone who would put together a setup like this would do to someone who tries to back out?*

He took a deep breath, staring at his tremoring hands until the shaking subsided. Then, still and calm as stone, he grabbed the handrail and walked down the stairs.

At the bottom was a simple wooden door. The wood itself was dark, maybe cherry but he wasn't sure. A white placard hung from a delicately filigreed brass and glass knob. In bright red block letters, it asked politely for him to "Please Come Inside." He turned the knob and pushed, but the door barely moved. He had to throw his shoulder against it, angling his feet into the carpet for traction and pushing with his thighs before it began to slowly swing inward.

The first thing that struck him about the room was how sterile it looked. How bland. The walls, floor, and ceiling were covered in stainless steel plating. The lights, bare tube fluorescents, were too bright. A man stood in the corner, clad in plain white scrubs along with a surgical mask and head covering.

The second thing that struck him was the screaming, mostly that he didn't notice it as soon as the door opened. Had it been going on the entire time? It had to have been.

Someone was strapped to a gurney in the center of the room. A naked man, so pale as to nearly fade into the blinding white of the room. He was the one screaming, his head thrown back and thrashing back and forth. The straps must have been secured tightly, as none of the rest of him appeared to move at all.

Celestin's feet moved forward, almost of their own accord. The man in the corner was silent. Or perhaps he was speaking, but could not be heard over the incessant noise. He stood still, pointing over at the man on the gurney. Specifically, at the lower half that ended a couple feet sooner than it should have.

"Shouldn't there be more blood?" Celestin stated absently as he stared at the knife laying down beside the stump that had been a left leg. Clamps and rubber tubing stuck out of the raw meat end of it. It was greyer than he expected. It should be red. Bright, screaming Argento red.

He shouldn't have been shaking, either. At least, not like this. Maybe with anger or misplaced hate. Not with fear. Still, he grabbed the knife. Gripped it tight, hoping the extra pressure would calm the shakes. For a moment, the man on the gurney looked into his eyes and stopped screaming. He didn't speak. Didn't beg or plead. Not with his voice. His eyes spoke volumes, though. In their busted capillaries and the raw red rings of his eyelids. In the pupils, dilated to yawning black gulfs of despair. Celestin tried to slow his breathing, his heart rate, just like he'd always done, but it wasn't working. Neither Eastern monk nor Western priest had a chant or a litany for this.

So, Celestin did what he knew. He ate. He tried his best to cut around any pieces that appeared to have something vital attached to them in the exposed portion of the stump. The knife was sharp and slid through the flesh smoothly. He couldn't be sure with the surgical mask in the way, but the man in the corner appeared to smile at this. The one on the gurney resumed his screams.

He shaved off a small sliver of meat and held it to his nose. He had heard somewhere that smelling almonds was a bad thing, but couldn't think of what almonds smelled like. The man in the corner winked at him as he placed it in his mouth.

The sensation hit him immediately, like lightning. Much more powerful and immediate than anything he had experienced before. No flashes of debauchery and cruelty or even a side glance at a neighbor's daughter's breast in a bikini top. Just blinding, searing light and heat filling him. Burning out everything he was.

The white light of heavenly grace, a soft voice from an old film briefly echoed in his skull before being burned away to nothingness. As the flames receded, they left scattered ashes of other lives in their wake. Simple moments. A hand outstretched, placing a twenty-dollar bill in a cheap plastic cup that rattled with change. A door held open. Soft, calming words slipping out into the dark over sobs. Arms wrapped around other arms in a mass of undulating yearning, not just in the greed of animal lust but in desperate shared need. And laughter. So much bright, light laughter that it exploded from him as screams. His eyes opened on the now dull chemical light of the fluorescents.

And all he wanted to do was tear the throat out of something.

He looked down at the knife he still held in his hand. Watched as his hand did its work. On its own at first, but he felt his own connection to it growing. This was him, now. No one else. No one to pass the impetus along to. His own mind and his own flesh that drove it into the chest of the man on the gurney, directly into his heart. The screaming stopped abruptly, as if turned off by a switch.

"Thank you," Celestin whispered into his ear, "for what you've given. I'm sorry it had to be like this."

There are times, boy, Father Bernard, always Father Bernard. That deep, gravelly voice groaning like the bones of the earth. *Times when mercy is not enough.*

The man in the corner was gesticulating wildly, his eyes wide and red above the mask. Celestin raised his free hand, palm flat, in the man's direction. He let go of the knife, leaving it embedded in the chest of the one on the gurney and reached across his face, gently closing his eyelids.

The man in the corner stood still, silent. His head moved back and forth in negation of the moment. His own hands went up in front of him.

"There's no point in begging now," Celestin's voice was calm, despite the hatred boiling inside his veins. "You've made your choices. It's time to pay for them."

At that, he let loose the bonds he had placed on his anger. Every bit of empty, impotent frustration he had sublimated into boredom came pouring out. With it, too, came the cries of two children who hadn't seen their father for a week. The tears of a wife and mother who knew, deep in her heart, none of them would see him again. The heart that broke, alone in a bland, blaring room that echoed with its screams. For the first time in his life, the rage he felt, both his and theirs, was truly righteous.

Times when you have to find those who have strayed from the beaten path...

He guided his hands through the work he had felt so often through others, aiming them. Gripping the throat with his left and squeezing, the muscles along his forearm shook with the exertion instead of fear or excitement. Something in the man's throat crunched and collapsed and his eyes bulged in their sockets.

Celestin slammed his right fist into the man's gut. Again and again and again, until the skin of his stomach split. He released his left hand, letting go of what little remained of the man's throat and reached into the hole left by his right. With both hands, he gripped skin and pulled outward, tearing it loose from ligature mooring and leaving the subdermal fat and musculature of the abdominal wall exposed.

The fat was swept aside easily enough, sliding and

sloughing off mostly on its own. The abdominal wall was a different story. The nail of his left ring finger snagged on the striations of muscle, ripping free, but he continued to dig at the dense tissue until it, too, opened a way to the blue and grey ropes of intestine beneath.

The man's chest still hitched, even with so much of himself turned inside out. A thin line of blood ran from the corner of his mouth. Somehow, this angered Celestin more. He wrapped the fingers of his left hand around the man's face, gripping the sundered remains of his throat with his right and lifted the man off the floor. With a raw, guttural scream, he slammed forward with both hands. Over and over, as if trying to punch the stainless walls through him.

...and beat them back onto it.

First, the skull gave. He expected something louder. The explosive crack of a bat or even the hefty crunch of a bag of ice thrown onto concrete. Instead, cushioned by skin and hair, it was quiet, almost apologetic. From there, the rest gave way easily. Red, grey and white smears streaked the wall. Shards of bone, pallid yellow in the fluorescent light, remained embedded in the metal. The body twitched twice and fell limp in his hands.

The rage slid away through the drain in the floor on the rivulets of blood, leaving Celestin drained but content. For a moment, he considered taking a taste, more out of habit than anything else. A mild curiosity about how those sins would stack up against the others he had devoured over the years. The urge and the curiosity passed quickly.

Professional Development

to: emp.all

from: Cyphere.Louis@WolfRamHartLlc.com

Dearest Employees, Underlings and Unpaid Interns,

While your valiant efforts and tireless dedication are always appreciated, the veritable cornucopia overflowing my inbox has made it clear that we are catastrophically close to experiencing a morale meltdown of practically biblical proportions. And you know how much I hate to throw around the B word at the office.

So, it appears that a little housecleaning is needed.

Because of this, we will be holding a series of non-workshops and monodirectional discussions. Attendance will, of course, be mandatory, regardless of your individual projects. See below for the itinerary:

9am: *Where the fuck are you?*: Seriously. We send hordes of stinging insects and particularly mucusy worms to your beds at 7am every morning. We know you are up. Is watching the fungus regrow over your toenails really interesting enough to spend the morning meditating over it? A reminder of policies and procedures re: tardiness.

10am: *The Ruttin' Chain I Beat You With Until You Follow My Commands*: The chain of command exists for a reason. Commands come on down from the lip of the fiery cliffs and any requests from you lowly saps are to crawl their way up from the bottom, over loops of barbed wire and links coated with the fat of unbaptized babies. A detailed list of all blank walls you may scream at instead of wasting my time pretending to care about what you have to say.

11am: *Well, bless you, Karen!*: Gesundheit. Excuse Me. Pardon my flatulence. Oh my, I appear to have crushed your hopes beneath the uncaring gaze of my tripartite lobes. Inappropriate communication has become a severe problem around the water cooler and at your desks. Puppet shows outlining proper language for you simpering fucking drool factories in slow, simple language that damned cocksuckers like yourselves can understand.

12 noon: break for lunch.

12:05pm: *Who ate my thrice damned Casu Marzu?* Just admit it. Just come forward and admit it. Own your mistakes and take your lashings or, so help me Samael, I will flay the skin from every single being in this office with the dullest of my toenails until someone rats you out. A placeholder because this happens every single blessed time.

12:30pm: *Let's all pretend we work on the deck of a cruise ship*. Team building exercise. Be sure to bring mops and buckets because, as it turns out, the removal of skin with an unsharpened appliance is a messy affair. Maybe you'll do a better job of policing each other next time.

1pm: *The Burning Book of Grammar and Elements of Soul,*

by Stunk and Wight: Far too many potential mail clerics and cold call sales associates are lost every millennium to poor sentence structure in the contract development department. A refresher on the importance of the Oxford Comma, who/whom distinctions and evolving pronouns so that those assholes in Divine Esotery don't stomp all over our own Ecclesiastical Pedantry department every fucking time.

2pm: *Keep it in your own heavenly ordained ears*: an hour straight of Alex Jones selling timeshares in Boca Raton and Tomi Lauren rambling on about whatever the heaven she is rambling on about this time until you get the point that nobody wants to hear Prairie Home Companion or Limp Bizkit or your 15th listen through The Purpose Driven Life and you use a pair of headphones. We bankrolled the expansion of Walmart down here for a reason.

3pm: *I know what cartoons you are sending to each other*: Too many of you don't seem to get that the email address we give you is for official, bringing-about-the-fall-of-man-and-eventually-the-almighty-himself business. Yes, I do monitor your emails. Yes, I know what you say about me and the other spawn you work with.

Now, so will they. A slide show of every stupid, catty email you write about each other. NAMES WILL BE PROVIDED.

4pm: *It's a bathroom, not a peep show*: If one more of you complains about so-and-so going into such-and-such bathroom then I will just ice down the whole place and beg on hands and knees to be reassigned back upstairs with the big toady himself. No one gives a fuck what fleshy appendage anyone did or did not have when they first birth forth from the fetid womb of their rancid progenitor. All of you exist in whatever form I allow you and none of you have any rights whatsoever anyways. Even down here, I don't have time for shitheads. I'll smack each of you in the face, then we will move on.

4:30pm: *There is no "I" in "Demonic Overthrow of Earth and Heaven"*. We're all here for the same reason. We all deal with the same celestial bullshit. It's about time we keep each other in mind, regardless of horn or tail length, throughout the day. Especially me, because I am sick of having to deal with your constant childish bickering and whining. So let's hold hands and mumble along to some classic Mayhem songs for our last half hour. Also, yes, I know that there is an "I" in "demonic" but I didn't feel like coming up with another word. Stop being so uptight, man.

5pm: *Fuck you. Good night*: I know I will be utterly done with all of you and your stupidity by the end of the day. So go home to your chains. Unwind over a nice pit of molten lava. Let the snap of whips and their sharp slip along your remaining flesh lull you to sleep before we dive back into the fray in the morning.

Debts of Generations Past, Come Due

"Just stop complaining, okay?" Beatrice said. Her voice echoed a bit too harshly from the rock walls. The smoke was in my eyes and I couldn't pinpoint her around the orange fire glow. "Just listen to the whispering, alright?"

"Yeah, bitch," Chad added. Fucker always had to add in something, especially when he didn't know what he was talking about. Still don't know why anyone invited him. I mean, yeah, he served a purpose, but he had never been anything but too much to deal with. Pineapple-spiked frosted tips, too-tight Tapout shirt and that date-rape sneer. Sure, I blew him in the upstairs gym alcove, but it was middle school. My taste was shit in middle school. "Don't get your panties, or whatever it is you've got tucked under that dress, in a twist."

"Shut up, C-Dizzle, Chizad or whatever it is you go by this week, before I stuff it with a few of these rocks," Damian said. He could be such a sweet guy when he wanted to be. I wished my eyes weren't watering from the carbon burn off so that I could catch a glimpse of those deep-set dimples one last time. It's a shame, what happened to him. He didn't deserve that shit. Even with the condescending tone he turned on me. "The Queen knows what she's doing."

The Queen. Fuck me running. Even in her full out retro-goth regalia, she still demanded to be referred to as her denied idol. Black lace from head to toe and a deeper ebony velvet swishing beneath it all. Let's not get into those clunky leather granny boots she bought online, then scored up to hell and back to fit the lie that they were the ones passed down from a gramma that had yet to pass into her dear, sweet Catholic heaven of serenading angels. Her skin powdered and brushed with pallid creams to the point of being the only thing not betraying a darker origin for her.

As if saying it was a Rice reference fooled people we grew up with in this too damn tight knit county. As if they didn't all know we were kin. As if her own slightly lighter daddy's gift of a creamier complexion meant a damn to the white hat warriors not so much hiding anymore. As if I couldn't hear the entirety of Lemonade rustling the old sheet that served to divide our rooms in the attic every fucking night.

"Okay," I relented. Respect to the elder was her due. "I just wish I could breathe a bit more. Maybe see clearer."

"The smoke helps the flavor, Ste-," luckily, our dearest Queen stopped herself short. I did what I could to direct the fallout of what our mother kept referring to as my ''lifestyle choice" away from her, regardless of how she annoyed me. The density of blood versus that of water and all. But she made it damn hard with how often she made me deal with the same bullshit from her. "Sephara.

"Think of it like a brick oven. Like at that place up in Dayton you like so much. Only the oven is much larger. Bigger. Whatever. The carbon doesn't just scorch the wheat; it soaks into it. It bonds to the fats in the cheese and alters every ingredient on the chemical level."

It was amusing how much she bought into her own line of bullshit. Maybe it helped her to pretend that it was all we were here for. Like the evening was actually going to end in something as mundane as a hilltop pizza party. I decided to ride with the lie, though.

"Also, we get the heady aroma of roasted bat shit," I couldn't help adding. I knew that would piss her off. Trivializing the

173

one thing she would admit to taking seriously. As much as I enjoyed the knowledge, as much as I relished the small victories where I could claw them from the rock-strewn soil of life, I needed this evening more. So I conceded her win and backed my assholish self off a bit. "The earthy tones of our mother's womb, I mean. Flavored with the gifts of her children, those beloved winged darlings of the night."

I tried to wink at Beatrice, but was sure it came out more as barely controlled contraction of swelling facial tics. There was no reason for this evening to be more successful in convincing her of my sincerity than any other.

Now was to be my part in the ritual. The one little bit I was allowed. Harmless as it was. The placement of toppings.

Sure, the boys selected them in advance. It was their role. A minor choice in the manner of their involvement. Not that either of them had to be asked. They were yelling out the preferred stylings of their end before Beatrice finished laying out the plans for the evening. Of course, they also immediately volunteered me to obtain their demanded treats before I could offer.

So, no, they knew nothing of the deep, forgotten ancestry of Leng in the bizarre, oblong arcs of the night-black olives, untouched by the purifying essence of ocean water. Nor were they cognizant of the Voormidarethian source of the sun-deprived shrooms I was so adamant were more potent than the shit-fueled, rubbery caps Chad grew in his closet. It goes without saying that I didn't bring up the finely ground meat of the mailman. Chester or Vinnie or whatever his name was that used to spend far too much time delivering his precious packages to the homes of dear young ladies in the lean hours between bus drops and parental arrival. Enough fennel and garlic cleanses the palate of such sins. Admittedly, the sauce was basic tomato paste from the local Genero-Mart. A girl can't do everything herself.

"Will you just throw it on, Sef," Chad, of course. That whining pestering masquerading as masculinity couldn't come from anyone else. I wanted to scream that there was a rhyme to follow here, a metre to the movements, just as I'd wanted to run him through with a spare dull blade since the offhand dismissal of *that stupid faggot* during freshman gym. I wanted a lot of things. Some were more important than others. "Who the fuck cares what it looks like? I wanna eat it."

"I'll do you a favor by not pointing out how much you hold to that ideal, dearheart. Some of us, though, take pride in our presentation."

Luckily, the motions were practiced to the point of pure muscle memory. Just like the Barishnikov dances I carried out behind the closed door of my elementary years. Repetition and practice and practicing repetitively into redundancy where everything from the tendons down to the individual protein fibers know the precise patterns of tension and release without electro-chemical inducement. The stinging burn of mucus membranes and the blurring of electromagnetic wavelength description of colors and shapes thankfully reduced to irrelevance.

Gramma, your great-gran that was, had always been particular about the importance of repetition. It was why she started me on crochet during those weekend trips that mom never joined us for. The same loops and hooks and pulls and stabs over and over and over again until the mind was not even needed. It wasn't until I mastered those that she moved me onto patterns of deeper import.

Thanks to this guidance, my fingertips knew to associate the earthy-spongy texture with linearity, with sharp non-Euclidean angles. Oily grit curved in spiral arcs and concentric non-spheres. Tiny circles held within circles of their own that slid between digits, a deeper dark of the desperate distances between those alien bits of sky-bound radiance, scattered as they wish amid the whims of Newtonian pull. Elements intricate and intrinsic in the ornate ornamental script spelling out names most dear to those who, naked, worship the night sky.

"There you go," I said, as an offer to the choking air as much as to Chad's idiotic essence and Damian's sweet unseen dimples and Beatrice's self-concerned arrogant grace.

Even in my non-vision, I could see the dough stretched across the bumps and divots of the marble slab. A symmetrically unnatural skull, so much more beautiful than the ugly, pitted and charred idols the fool and the prince would eventually leave stuck in the teeth of greater beasts than us all, that our dear Queen Bee bought with nought but a wink and a smile from a far too desperate Northside marble sculptress.

I could feel the yeast, lost in heat and suffocation, pushing out fluffed bubbles into the protein-bound, gluttonous ooze of their tomb. The fat of bovine lactate running, stretched and smooth, to viscous glue. The pink and grey and black dots and dashes glowing bright, pouring forth exponential degrees beyond that which was fed to them by the incinerated tree flesh.

"Do you hear that?" Beatrice said. I could hear the waver, the whimper just below the confident and secure surface. Even if none of the others noticed, I knew it was there. She knew her control had slipped. Somewhere, at some point she could not identify, it had escaped her.

Gramma had warned us about this moment. It was the point that mattered most. The point where our mother had failed so dreadfully. I'd always hated her a bit for that. Thought her weak, even. With the weight shifting ever so slightly beneath us, tipping us toward these bitter, terrible ends, I understood how she could suddenly throw her own back toward the bland commonplace. I still don't forgive her the cost of that decision, though.

"Hear?" The words flowed from Damian's lips.

He could be forgiven for mistaking that keening screech for the wind, the rapid exchange of interior hot air with the cool evening air outside. Damian was always among the first to excuse the usual mutterings and mumblings heard in the cave as the settling bones of the earth. He had no reason to believe, despite numerous discussions wherein I tried to convince him of the contrary, in the hidden doors on rusty, ill-used hinges. Let alone the long-neglected locks that were finally slipping free.

I just wish he had been smart enough to keep those foolish, gorgeously plump lips in place. Wasn't there supposed to be some part of the lizard brain that took over in times like this? Something that recognized the presence of a superior predator and shut down the nervous system?

Not that silence would have spared him in the end. There was a payment owed for knowledge granted. The old books were clear on that point. Your Great Gran was clearer. The delay in payment, the missed delivery our own blood had denied, got us into this mess in the first place. His life was forfeit the moment he hopped into the back of his beloved Queen's polished onyx Charger earlier in the evening. Maybe he could have avoided the greed and savagery of bellies that had gone unfilled for decades.

I could feel them more than see them. Even with the smoke cleared away into the drafts of the Small Spaces, the interior of the cave had grown darker. Still, the lymphatic, inside out sliding of those muscled appendages could not be missed. No more than the dry, frantic scratchings of claws against bare stone. Somewhere, untold rows of teeth gnashed and scraped against each other.

When they found Damian, still drooling that single, idiot word like old molasses, he didn't bother screaming. I want to believe him brave, stoic in the face of his own inevitable demise. It's more likely that his interior lizard showed up a little too late to do any good.

What followed was a flurry of loud, wet movements. A hyperactive blur of slicing and separating, of digging and dragging away. Of teeth no longer scraping against each other but dear Damian's bones. Something meaty slurped at the stones, removing any blood or small pieces of him that remained.

Through it all, I kept my head tilted downward, the steepled thumbs, forefingers, and pinkies pressed to my heart, throat, and skull. The odd angle made proper enunciation of the invocation significantly more difficult. Fixating on the thickness of the words, the overabundance of consonants and dorsal/glottal stoppages helped keep my mind detached, at least.

Chad was the lucky one. Of course he was. He'd always been, so why would now be any different?

I could hear him moaning over my own muttering. His clothes falling softly to the floor as the moist tendrils slithered over him, drawing out the moment now that the desperation of its hunger had abated. Several names slipped from his lips, sighed out into the air. I'm pretty sure I heard my own among them, but that may well have been wishful thinking. Don't give me that look. We all want to be remembered, even if it is by idiots and assholes.

The moans ceased abruptly as the caresses shifted to constriction. His bones popped and snapped under the increased pressure. I'd always assumed that the cliched comparison to dry sticks to be an idiotic one, but it fit here. If those sticks were first coated in mud and wrapped around the moldering carcass of a long-passed raccoon.

All respect due to Chad, the dude never screamed. I know that the blood pressure is supposed to pop your brain to mush way before anything else, but it still seems like there would be a lot of pain involved. Nothing but that soft whisper of air escaped him, carrying with it the names of all his past fucks.

With the screaming and moaning faded into the smoke, the cave became significantly quieter. I could hear Beatrice's voice again. She was muttering something that didn't hold the cadence of the chant our grandmother had drilled into our skulls. It was irregular. Panicked.

"Sorry... never... I," she stammered. I couldn't make out all the words. What I could make out lacked the Queenly grace she almost always commanded. "Not... fault... theirs..."

It sounded suspiciously like begging. Not something I had ever heard from her. The girl, later the woman, I had never heard shudder. Not in the slightest, regardless of the circumstances. She was The Queen. Others feared her. That was the way it had always been.

The stone around us quaked in answer to her pleas. Not words. Words were too abstract for a being like this. A meaningless bauble meant for children. This was much more immediate in effect, more visceral.

It was not pleased.

I wanted to run to her. Despite the years of condescension and cruel laughter, I wanted to throw myself between it and her. That was the way such things were supposed to go. The younger, fragile one sacrificed for the good of the elder, the stronger. It was what allowed the spheres to fall back onto their usual axis.

It wouldn't do any good, though. I knew it as well as I knew the hitch of my own breath. There were rituals and rights to be observed. They had been broken. Breaking them further would appease nothing.

Hunger and lust had been sated. Certainly. They were a due debt. This was different. Promises were made. They were not kept. Even when we told ourselves otherwise, we knew how this would play out.

I continued with the invocation, repeating the litany over and over. I retreated further into the words, into the intricacies of the alien syllables that made them up. Each time increasing volume until it felt like my throat would burst. Hoping that noise, if nothing else, could deny what was occurring mere feet away from me.

Who knows how long I remained like that. An idiot child shouting nonsense into the choking void. It felt like hours. Perhaps days. Most likely, it was just a few minutes. My throat was raw and my eyes burned and my hands ached. I wanted to cry when I felt a thin, ooze covered tendril draw itself down from the tip of my nose, across the center of my lips, in a mockery of a well-known gesture.

"Shhhh, now," it didn't speak, but still said. "Quiet and calm yourself."

Another tendril, thicker and more muscular, pressed down gently on my shoulder. My legs gave out and I fell to my knees.

The jagged rocks on the floor of the cave did not treat them kindly and the pain brought a sharpness to my senses. I lifted my head up, proud in my own way. I'd remembered the face of my grandmother and held to the ritual when it mattered most. Whatever happened from here would be what needed to happen.

Slick, sharp teeth scraped along the side of my neck, sending shivers through me. Something thin pierced my throat in the divot between muscle and larynx. The sweet spot where life flows.

Immediately, my brain exploded with flashes of lightning and insight. I could see it all playing out before me: How to solve so many of our stupid, consumptive problems. Simple, elegant paths to seed our future with joy and prosperity without drawing too much attention from those outside.

Such visions were promised. They were part of the deal, the return on our investment, so to speak. I was not prepared for what followed.

Behind my eyes, I saw rivers of the same well-muscled tendrils spill from the mouth of the cave. Each one ended in a circular, pulsing mouth that flexed, flashing row upon row of glistening, razor-edged teeth, as they undulated down towards town. Friends and neighbors and family screamed as they did their work, rending and chewing and swallowing. Each one whispering my name to its victim before leaping to feast. The point was clear.

"Understood?" it again distinctly did not say.

"Yes," I responded, doing my best to feign calm. As if it wasn't already inside me and couldn't read every thought.

"Thirty years. No more. No less."

I thought of you then, the daughter I didn't yet have. The years of practice that would be needed. The dedication and perseverance. The weight that had been shouldered by so many of our forebears laid onto you without even the opportunity of consent. I hoped then, as I do now, that you would understand.

"We will not fail you again," I promised.

If You Were Dreaming, You'd Know

in the name of Tony and Pat and the haunts that aren't quite ghosts

Jennifer was crying out again. Screaming at the top of her lungs that she wanted to play. That she wanted to go outside under the big blue sky and feel the last of the evening sun wash over her face. She wanted to roll in the grass, even if she was always itchy afterwards. They could run through the sunflowers and breathe in their sweet aroma. Maybe they could sneak into the Richards' yard and eat some of their black berries from the bush right on the edge of the property. Nobody would know. Besides, it was sooooooo boring sitting here on the couch watching the news.

Agnes knew they couldn't do any of that. They couldn't steal blackberries that hadn't grown in years. She knew the sunflowers were nothing more than brittle, brown stalks, dry and dead in the earth. Knew that the grass was overgrown and full of too many weeds for a proper roll and romp. She knew that the sun just didn't shine so bright anymore. Just as she knew Jennifer could neither eat, smell, run, roll, feel, or scream. Not anymore. Not for too many years to count now.

She *knew* these things, but she wanted so much to believe. Wanted to believe Jennifer hadn't been planted underneath those sunflowers well before her time. Wanted to believe that she honestly didn't believe an old Raggedy Ann doll was talking to her with her dear baby girl's voice. Telling her that they could swing from the stars together.

Robert used to be so good at helping her through this. He'd rub her back and talk to her about what was on the news that night. Tell her about the neighbor boy who needed help getting his lawnmower working after he ran it into a stump like a fool. Take her out to sit in their bench under the oak tree that had been there since before they owned the place. Hold her hand and make her feel solid again. Bring her back to the now. Bring her body back in control of her soul, or the other way around.

She almost called out for him. Almost began a frantic search through the house for the man who had stood by her side through those years. The man who held her up and held her together. The one who stopped her when she said she was going out to buy groceries but was really planning on walking into the lake down the hill. Who told her there was nothing they needed all that badly and he'd much rather spend the night with his arm around his beautiful lady.

But she remembered he wouldn't answer. Not anymore. They'd come and taken him away from her. They were supposed to help. She remembered that much. Remembered that they were supposed to make him better. But they just carted him away mumbling a bunch of nonsense she couldn't understand and shaking their heads.

They still hadn't brought him back. She had to go to the grey garden near town without him. No one to hold her hand and sway with her to the songs. No one to giggle in her ear about the silly, pointless things the man in black said. She had to ride home with someone she was sure she should recognize but couldn't. Robert was supposed to remind her, but he couldn't.

She didn't want the neighbors coming over, that nice young couple who took over after the Richards left. They seemed so worried the last time. They asked her if she needed any help and didn't seem to believe her when she said she was fine. She just forgot, for a moment, that Robert was away. Being taken care of. She did ask if they could take her to visit him, but they said it was too late at night for that. Looked at her like a bug in a jar. Like they were frightened of her. She just told them to leave, thanking them all the while.

So she calmed herself down. She needed to do something about Jennifer, though. That screaming was bound to bring someone. Some fool would think she was torturing the girl, instead of it just being another temper tantrum. Maybe she'd have to give her what she wanted. Take her outside for a little bit. After all, kids needed a chance to be kids every once in awhile.

The girl was too light. Too limp in her arms. Agnes decided that she needed to eat more. Maybe she'd make her up some chicken soup in the morning. That was just the thing to put a bit of meat back on her. The trick was to use the skin in the broth. Some said it made the soup too greasy, but the fat was what put meat on our bones. She'd learned that from her own mother.

In the meantime, she carried Jennifer outside, singing a weakened tune through weakened lungs. The graveyard night shining with stars like wounds in a great black sheet. They must've missed the sun while she fretted over a decision she knew would be made for her anyways. They could still walk down to the lake, though. Jennifer always liked to watch the moon rise, reflected in the water.

It was a pity Robert wouldn't come down, too. It made him uncomfortable. He told her, once, that the lake was filled with tears and that he couldn't bear to think of all the agony it took to fill it. Worse, he said, was the thought of all the tears yet to be cried. The knowledge that they'd overrun the shore and drown them all one day.

She giggled to herself, deciding that she'd have to make him some chamomile tea to calm himself down once they got done playing in the water.

What Grows Inside

written with Piper Morgan

Two lines shouldn't mean this much. Hell, the second was barely visible. Two tiny strips of pink on a field of merciless white. It didn't make sense. Emersen blinked and took a breath, not realizing that she had been holding her lungs in suspension while she waited for the nothing she wanted to appear. The rush of oxygen cleared her head a bit. Enough for the dull eggshell of the plastic to come into focus and the ammonia sting of urine to aggravate her nose. Enough to steady her eyes and look at the stick again.

Every bit of her hoped she was wrong. Her eyes playing games, imagining the second strip. *Just like you imagined it on the other three?* An invasive, arrogant voice chimed in her head. *Might as well hold onto the dream.*

Nope.

Still the same half-assed attempt at an equation, only without the numbers on either end. Just the implication of X plus Y equaling Z, wherein the X is a little backroom bump and tickle, the

Y standing in for momentary carelessness and Z... Well, Z is becoming pretty damn clear now, isn't it?

"MOTHERFUCK!" It wasn't a scream. Not quite, not yet, but she could feel it building up inside of her. The pressure expanding her lungs to near bursting.

Her hands shook. The Early Answer One Step ("Get a jump start on your new life!") was on the floor. At some point, she had dropped it. Maybe she threw it down. She couldn't remember. Now, it sat there, face up and mocking her with those faint pink lines. Hot tears rolled down her cheeks and her stomach churned, making her wish she hadn't eaten that late breakfast.

It was all her sister's fault. Not the... Emerson couldn't bring herself to name it. Not her *condition*. Emersen knew the cause of that well enough, but she'd always been careful. This *thing*, this parasite inside of her, was the last thing she wanted. It was just supposed to be a harmless weekend trip up to the mountains. A way to blow off steam, since both of them had been stressed with their jobs. A surprise vacation on Lauryn's tab. Plane tickets, rental car, and motel all taken care of. Emersen didn't think to throw in the birth control with the rest of her stuff. She hadn't even bothered packing shampoo or soap. It was just a few days, after all. There hadn't been any point in worrying about it. What was the worst a few days off could do?

This, apparently.

Nine months bound to a malignant growth. Watching it grow and squirm just beneath the surface. For a moment, she wondered if the churning in her stomach was that thing, that IT, rolling around in her innards like a pig in a mud puddle. The image of a pink, bean-like being clawing translucent fingers through uterine lining to get at the ropes of intestine and lumpy, purplish bags of kidney overrode any sense of logic. The other side of that equation and the worst news she'd ever received in her life.

She walked into the kitchen and stood on the other side of the pale oak finished table from Jesse. Her eyes followed the whorl and spin of the knots. They rode the irregular waves of the grain from one end to the other, sliding their way back down the harsh, straight lines where separate pieces were joined together. They spun around a circle of condensation at the base of a glass of sweet tea, prompting her to think, for what was likely the twentieth time, about how they needed to start using coasters so that they didn't ruin the finish. They bobbed along with the neon lemon slices floating in the brown liquid as they danced around the melting ice cubes. They bounced among the miscellaneous squiggles, loops and lines of black on dull grey that made up the silly eight-page rag that dared call itself a community newspaper without making sense of any of them. But her eyes didn't meet Jesse's. Couldn't.

She took a deep breath and thought about the five years she and Jesse had been together. Longer than her own parents had been when she was born. Her mom had already started the slow, not so gentle push for a quiet ceremony at the family church. The push that Emersen knew would lead to the mention of grandkids soon enough. When she told Jesse about it, he started laughing right away. The subject of tiny, squalling lumps that demanded everything in wordless screeches while they siphoned out every last bit of life to feed their insatiable greed had come up often enough between them. He always giggled along with her, but never said anything more than that.

"Let's take a walk," she said. Her voice didn't sound like her. At least, it didn't sound like she thought she should sound right now. It was even. It was calm. It was blandly conversational. Every nerve was strung tighter than piano wire and her mouth was able to play along as if her world wasn't crashing to pieces around her. She almost laughed.

Jesse looked up at her from the half-page interview with the new member of the volunteer firefighters. She focused on the individual wiry hairs that made up his eyebrows to keep from looking into his eyes. "Why?"

"It's a nice day," she said. The last word hit an unexpected high note, as if desperate to leap from her mouth. The panic was starting to creep into her voice. She tried to tamp it down. "Why not?"

He glanced at the SPCA calendar hanging on the pale yellow walls. A golden retriever ran through a field of tall grass in the image for the month. Long, yellow fur flew along its flank. Its mouth hung open in a slack, doofus grin that bespoke absolute canine joy. It wasn't wearing a collar. "Because it's August?"

Emersen tried to swallow around the lump of fear in her throat and blew out the breath she had been holding. *You can do this,* she tried to reason with herself. Her interior voice was nowhere near as good at pulling off the trick as the exterior. *It'll only be for a little bit. Twenty minutes, tops.* She wasn't sure if she was talking to him or to herself when she finally said, "I'm sure it'll be fine."

Jesse arched a dark eyebrow, furrowing half of his forehead in the process. "You never want to go out during the summer." He stared at her face, trying to catch her eyes. Trying to read his future in the lines of her face, perhaps. His own was blank. "What's up?"

She shook her head. He knew well enough that it wasn't being outside that was the problem. She loved the feeling of the sun warming her skin. The soft brush of the wind, or even its rough grasp as a storm rolled in. Even wracked by allergies, she lived for the heady, heavy scent of air thick with pollen and humidity filling her sinuses until they slammed themselves shut. It was taller grass and the unkempt shrubbery so many of their neighbors let run rampant over the sidewalks, not to mention the thick underbrush that filled in between the trees and overran the trails through the woods, that she didn't trust. She knew what hid there, waiting patiently to dig into any uncovered, accessible skin.

She rushed to the sink and turned on the tap. The stainless steel felt cool against her overheated skin as she leaned over to splash her face with icy water. The panic was cloying, threatening to choke her. She knew she could do this. It was just a matter of actually getting outside. Once she was at the edge of the woods, she could force herself to put one foot in front of the other. Maybe the constant, mundane fear would cancel out the terror of the moment and she could get this over with.

Emersen heard rustling paper and the chair scraping over the old, faded linoleum before Jesse came to stand behind her, lightly rubbing her back. His touch was making her edgy and the fresh cut cedar and tobacco scent of him enveloped her, invading her nose and mouth. Normally, she liked breathing him in, reveling in the associated sense of love and comfort. At just this moment, though, it was too much. As it was, she barely held the line in the fight against the tears that threatened to burst from her burning eyes. The gorge rising from her gut would be too much to bear, even if she'd already vomited too much for anything else to come up.

She pushed herself from the sink and shrugged his hands off her. She didn't hear his feet on the cheap vinyl flooring, so she knew he wasn't following her as she walked over to the open screen door. Fresh, warm air blew around her and she inhaled deeply, the sweet, musky smell of the dogwood out back forcing Jesse's scent from her lungs. She took a couple of calming breaths. The ancient, careless calm of the larger world flowed in and out of her with each of them. Finally, she turned toward him.

"I'm pregnant," she blurted.

The two words were simple enough. They were what all of this had added up to. Yet, they seemed to hold more weight than their total value. Enough to drop Jesse's jaw to the floor.

He froze, his face a stupid, dumb mask. As if the sound waves had slapped him and stalled his brain with the impact. Time dilated. She felt like she could have lived three or four lives in the spaces between his own breaths. Innumerable dawns and dusks passed around them. Whole civilizations rose and fell. He pursed his lips and swallowed, his Adam's apple bobbing in his throat. He walked toward her and smiled, holding out his hand.

"How about that walk then?"

***

"Get it off me!" Emersen's screams echoed through the trees. The frantic sounds of flapping wings and angry screeches followed.

She could feel the tiny setae sliding, whisper soft, over her skin. Then, the sharp prick of the hypostome, parting cells to probe at the warm fluid that pulsed beneath. She was certain of the sensation of suction in the crook of her elbow. Her veins felt hollower by the second. Some distant, oddly calm portion of her mind wondered how much of this they could take before collapsing completely.

Beside her, Jesse laughed.

Her vision blurred, eyes covered in a thin sheen of tears before they finally broke, streaming down her cheeks. "Jesse, please." She was begging. She hated every second of it. Hated this feeling of weakness and dependence. Hated the expression of it even more. It made her feel small and helpless, but none of that stopped her.

"Oh, for Christ's sake." He mumbled, rolling his eyes as he grabbed her wrist. The movement was rough, a touch angry. Her tendons strained when he pulled her toward him. His other hand went to the simple leather holster at his side. She remembered buying it for him the year before, the wide smile on his face as he took in the tiara clad manatee burned and dyed into the side. He unsnapped the strap and removed the tiny knife, held it against her arm. Emersen had enough time to note how cool the blade was against her skin before he scraped the thing away in a smooth motion.

The engorged brown spot rested on the edge of the blade,

the steel now covered in a deep crimson. He put his cigarette out on the spot, its body squirming and sizzling before finally popping. Jesse wiped the blade off on his bandana as Emersen collapsed onto the ground, sharp twigs poking at her legs through the material of her jeans.

With her good arm, the arm that wasn't shriveled and infected, she upended her bag. The mess was a jumble of nonsense on the muddy ground. A pile of day-to-day detritus held together by half-melted candy and old, wadded tissue paper. Still, she quickly found what she was looking for. The small clear tube was nearly empty, but it would work until she could get to the house. She flipped open the lid with her thumb and squeezed the remaining gel on her open wound.

The smell of alcohol filled the air. The hole in her arm burned. It was a great fire, seeping in through the wound to sterilize whatever foulness that disgusting abomination had left in her. She hoped it would be enough.

"Are you done yet?"

Her head snapped to the left, so fast that a sharp pain shot through her neck. She winced and glared at him. His crooked smile was irritating. The image of her fist smashing into the smug grin flooded her mind. *How the hell can I love someone so much, but still want to smash his face in?* she thought, forcing a tight smile.

"You know, for someone who prides herself on being tough, you sure are a pussy."

"Fuck you, Jesse McKay!"

She stomped through the woods towards civilization and the comfort of lifeless concrete. His laughter, high and cruel, followed her along the trail. It felt like the leaves and trees were propagating it, amplifying the sound to reach her no matter how far away she went.

This walk was supposed to be relaxing. A nice jaunt in the beauty of nature to take her mind off the thing growing inside of her. If she'd known that the park hadn't gotten around to trimming down the weeds growing up over the trail, she would have suggested something else. Her first instinct was to turn back when she saw the state of it. Jesse was in such a good mood, though. Someone needed to be. So she pushed down her misgivings and went on in. The worst day of her life was just getting worse.

She glanced down at her arm, not wanting to see it but knowing she'd just obsess if she didn't look. The puncture wound was raised and bright red. A thick, milky fluid oozed out of the hole the beast had made. Her skin felt hot and tight. The arm looked shorter than it should be. She held her arms together. Yep, the infected one was definitely shrinking. It had to be at least a centimeter shorter than its twin.

Emersen wanted to scream. She wanted to curl up into a ball on her bed and weep uncontrollably. The idea of taking each and every one of the spare pain meds the two of them had built up over years was particularly attractive at the moment. Maybe all three were in order.

Not only did she have this hopeless squalling lump inside of her, now she had a tick bite. Maybe even Lyme disease. She tried to remember if the bright red, suppurating spot on her arm had the telltale bullseye pale ring or not. The more she thought about it, the more certain she became that it was true. Even if it wasn't, there was always ehrlichiosis. Her muscles did feel unusually sore. Possibly Rocky Mountain spotted fever. Her head was pounding. Would she wake up in a few days, covered in raised, red welts? She could break lucky enough to be the first recorded case of some new, as of yet unnamed disease that was caused by getting attacked by ticks and getting the worst news of your life on the same day. They could name it after her. She'd be in all the papers. Pictures of her holding her new unwanted guest in her only remaining arm would be recorded for posterity and the viewing pleasure of audiences worldwide.

***

"Have you felt the baby kick yet?" asked Lauryn, putting her hands on Emersen's growing belly. No permission was asked. No one ever bothered asking. They just groped away, as if she existed purely for them to poke and prod and fondle.

She'd always had issues with being touched. Even as a child, she'd felt violated whenever someone, usually a particularly invasive aunt or family friend, wrapped her in a rushed and unwanted embrace. Since she started showing, it had become intolerable. Everyone thought they had some right to her skin just as the thing inside of her had claimed a right to her innards.

"I'm trying to ignore it. It doesn't bother me. I don't bother it."

Her sister laughed, the cheerful sound filling the small room. It was as bright and as sickening as the loud floral print dress she wore. The damn thing was so bright that it should have come with a battery pack. An attempted symbolic reminder of the riot and fecundity of spring instead of the reminder of the weed-ridden spewing of pollen and other allergies that it actually was. "It's not an IT, it's your baby boy. A beautiful creature that you're going bring into this world."

"Creature sounds about right." Emersen pulled away from Lauryn's hands. She did her best to mask it by straightening herself up on the couch, readjusting a spine under constant duress from the beast taking her over. Still, Lauryn's face twisted into a grimace of mixed pain and annoyance for a fraction of a second.

"Oh, stop. It's a wonderful experience."

"That's what you keep telling me. If I had the couple thousand bucks and a couple days to take off for the five hour trip up north to the one damn clinic in our state, I wouldn't have this..." She pointed down before flopping her hands to her sides.

"Emersen!"

There wasn't any reason to be surprised by Lauryn's reaction. Her eyes lit up like twin suns when Emerson, hands shaking and eyes overflowing, told her. Just like everyone else she knew, so full of vicarious joy for her *blessing*. It made her feel grotesque, monstrous, when she looked at the slippery wooden staircase leading to the bare concrete slab of the basement. A desperate longing for the release in a simple giving over to gravity was held in those simple slats. Only the thought of her terrible luck had the power to still her foot the two or three times a day she found herself at that precipice. She had a vivid image of herself, strung up in traction, with every bone in her body broken but with that damnable thing unharmed in any meaningful way, screaming while it tore itself through her and out into the world. The thought was still enough to scare her away from the stairs.

"Well, it's true," Emersen looked down at her hands. Clearly, there was something wrong with her. Something fundamentally inhuman that forced these thoughts, this refusal to accept her biologically predetermined destiny. The shock and denial she received from everyone only served to hammer the point in. "No point in lying about how I feel. As soon as it's born, I'm putting it up for adoption."

"You'll change your mind once my little nephew is in your arms."

She watched her sister's face at the mention of her arms, but she just kept talking. It was nothing more than an expected, empty platitude to her. Emersen looked down at her shrunken and wrinkled left arm, at the perfect, angry crimson circle in its crook. The spot where the hypostome had pierced her skin hadn't healed. It was still marked with a pallid green, oozing head. No matter how often she scrubbed and disinfected, it never went away. It only seemed to get worse.

Why wasn't she saying anything? she often wondered. Lauryn made a point of taking diligent care of Emersen since the pregnancy had been announced. Always demanding to be the one driving Emersen to her OBGYN appointments, sitting next to her the entire time and asking far more questions than Emersen had any desire to have answered. She was the one monitoring everything Emersen ate and pushing her to keep up on her exercises, even when all she wanted to do was hide under her covers and pretend it would all go away on its own.

Lauryn was the first one to notice the growing, dark bags under her eyes. She jumped all over every cough and sneeze as if they were the first sign of the end of the world. She didn't mince any words when she felt Emersen was gaining too much weight, no matter how much she knew it would affect her sister. It didn't make any sense that she would ignore such an obvious and terrifying problem.

The doctor wasn't any better. Doctors. Between her GP, the OBGYN, and the preliminary meetings with the pediatrician Lauryn had also demanded she see, she spent at least one day a week in some glaringly white office or another. Yet, none of them mentioned any issues or concerns. When she finally broke down and started asking them, they just looked confused. Each face scrunched up in identical lumps of confounded wrinkles. Outside of the weight gain that everyone seemed so damn concerned with, as if she didn't have an abnormal growth inside of her that was bound to increase her mass by no insignificant degree, they couldn't see anything wrong with her.

"Sure," Dr. Vasquez, the OBGYN, told her, "your arms are a bit bloated, but that is just from the water retention. If you would just cut down on your sodium intake, like I've asked you to do for the past three times I've seen you, then you'd see an improvement. The redness is just high blood pressure, which could also be fixed by the same thing and maybe a bit more exercise."

She rolled her eyes and inwardly snorted.

Swelling?! It's half its original size and looks like a deflated balloon. That is not fine. I am not fine. Nothing is fine. Something got into me when that segmented, disgusting creature latched on. It took out my blood and left something in its place. I'm infected, possibly infested.

She felt something flutter, just behind the now prominent outward nub of her belly button. The sensation of motion beneath her skin turned her stomach. The lizard core of her brain reacted instinctively, trying its best to force out whatever had invaded her in a series of harsh retches. Unfortunately, she knew well enough that no voiding of her gullet or bowels would do the job. If that worked, she'd have been rid of it much earlier.

"Oh! He's moving, isn't he?" Lauryn grabbed Emersen's hand, the right one, of course. No one in their right mind would touch the abomination of her left arm. Before Emersen could react, she found it placed on her belly.

The fluttering gave way to rolling and she tried to yank her hand away in revulsion. If this was what every pregnant woman went through, she didn't understand why the human race continued growing so rapidly. Her sister's hand on hers was steel though. It had transmuted into a vice that refused to let go.

"No, wait, this is awesome."

Awesome to who? Emersen thought. *What kind of person*

would be enveloped by a sense of awe at the preparatory motion of a parasite readying itself to burst into the world?

The rolling turned into a push. The sensation, along with everything it intimated, was enough for Emersen's hand to break Laryn's inhuman hold. She jerked it away and held it above her head, keeping it as far away from the IT inside of her as she could.

Her retching gave way to a cold sweat. She'd gone thirty years without ever touching a pregnant woman's stomach. The pride in giving over precious internal real estate had never sat well with her. It was an immoral violation she would never allow anyone else. It never made sense to suddenly be okay with such an invasion purely because of a shared genetic coding. It was a record she was not only fine with, but quite proud of. Just another thing that had been taken away from her by someone else.

"Isn't it wonderful?"

No, her immediate thought, even if she lacked the heart to state it. *This is the worst thing I have ever experienced in my life.*

It was too much for her to deal with. The ruin of her arm, the growth that wriggled and writhed within her, and this determination that she should be so damn excited about all of it.

The convulsing of her abdomen won out over propriety and the spaghetti, sauce, meatballs, cheese, and all she'd eaten for lunch came up in a slow lurch. It bulged and fell from her mouth before falling in wet, red clumps onto the linoleum and Lauryn's pretty, pretty flowers.

***

"One more push."

The harsh fluorescent light hurt her eyes. The gown and sheets were scratchy. She wanted to gag at the antiseptic stench of the room. Her sweaty hair was matted against her face. The pillow was lumpy and the fact that she was turning her head back and forth on it wasn't helping. Jesse and Lauryn kept spewing unintelligible rivers of vowels without consonants. The nurse and the doctor were no better. Everything they said was muffled by cotton swaths that covered their mouths. The noise, the grating, all of it was pissing her off.

She clamped down on Jesse's hand. "No."

"Come on, Em. It's almost over."

Emersen squeezed her eyes shut, white tracers floating behind her closed lids. "No."

Something wasn't right. Something beyond the usual Not

Right of the whole damn situation. Something they didn't cover in any of the hours-long consultations and checkups and consultations about the checkups.

There was pain. Not the *holy shit, my whole lower half is contracting in on itself and something is ripping me in half from the vagina upwards* pain she was told to expect. It wasn't coming from the right places. It wasn't the right kind of pain. Her blood boiled. It rushed through her veins with the force of a rocket. Thousands of tiny needles jabbed into her clammy skin. Suction and pressure built up inside of her.

"Come on Emersen." The doctor peeked up from between her thighs. Even with the white cloth covering the lower half of his face, she could see the grin splitting it. How anyone could smile through the ruin that was befalling her parts, she couldn't understand. "One more push."

"No!" she screamed. Her head pounded and her skin was on fire. Her stomach flipped and flopped. Her arm pulsated. The skin of it was stretched as tight and shiny as plastic wrap. Surely it would rip from the pressure at any moment.

"Em, you've wanted this day to come for a while." Jesse's breath forced its way into her ear. "One more push and it'll be over."

"I can't, Jesse," she cried. "I don't feel right. Something is..." She screamed and grasped his hand, squeezing as hard as she could. The hurried beeps of the heart monitors were drowned out by the screams that echoed off the pale gray walls.

The pain she was expecting finally hit. Razors scraped down from her uterus. Intense pressure and tearing skin. Her legs being forced open at unnatural angles. Muscles and tendons ripped free from bones in a series of pops and tears. The sharp crack of her pelvic bone snapping echoed off the walls. Biology and evolutionary imperative gave her no choice but to push.

She looked down to a crimson stain spreading over the once white sheet used to hide the ruin of the flesh between her legs. Even in the heart of this storm of whirling, screaming agony, she dimly noted the sensation of bristly legs brushing up against the inside of her thighs. Far too many of them.

The doctor rose up from behind the sheet. That same sick grin was stretched beneath the cotton. His eyes were bright, glowing with accomplishment. In his arms, he swaddled an oblong, oddly flat shape that squirmed and struggled in the fluffy, white towel wrapped around it. While she couldn't see the face, she could make out a brown, thick protrusion emerging from where the head should be in the towel. A sharp, barbed protrusion. Something that would be perfect for piercing skin and slurping away the thick, red blood beneath the surface. It vibrated with a shrill cry.

"It's a boy," she could hear Jesse say through the screen of her own screams. "A perfect baby boy.

One Time Would Be Enough

They didn't see her. Or hear her. Somehow, they never did. Her joints were tight and creaky with arthritis and rot. Grave dirt and maggots didn't do any wonders to connective tissue, after all. She'd been their age once, blinded to damn near everything by the heat and need between her legs, but she hoped she would have noticed the dry glass against concrete scrape of bone on bone. On the plus side, she could always console herself with the lie that they deserved it.

She waited through their howls and frenzied rutting. Watched the rusted steel coils give and flex as cheap nylon threading bulged towards her, then back. The rage built inside of her with each bounce of careless flesh, so like the waves pulsing against the shore all those years ago. The promise to let them finish, to let them find some final joy barely stayed her hand.

When he left, and yes, it was always he who left, she'd slip around and over. Put her full weight onto the forehead and hold the girl still while the right hand did its work. A piston punching sliver-thin holes in her chest as the girl's mouth opened wide, spilling screeds of a thousand unknown final tongues.

The scream cut short in mid-whimper, air wheezing its way out of punctured lungs and a ruined trachea. Blood bubbling, viscous and black in the moonlight. Folds of flesh flopped and rubbed against each other in steadily decreasing fury. The deep crimson flames overflowing her vision receded.

Still, there were the eyes. The eyes always did her in. So full of surprise and confusion that all Pamela wanted to do was hold them in her arms while they slipped away.

So she did.

And she remembered the same look in her baby's eyes all those years ago when she couldn't force enough air past the slimy lake water that gummed up his lungs to get them working again. When she'd wrenched her shoulders doing her best to flat-palm press his heart back to beating. When they'd stopped rolling around wildly. When the wheezing had stopped and all that was left was the dry scrape of shattered bones scraping against each other in his chest. When the tendons holding her elbow tight gave way and she just saw his face rushing up towards hers through the screaming tears.

Sirens and hands and voices, so many voices all tangled together, measured the flow of time. Time didn't matter anymore, though. In that moment, she had transcended whatever nonsense Einstein spouted, propelled by the gyre of her grief past known physics. Not that she knew it then.

Even when she found herself on the same shore, in the same spot, blood staining the creases of knuckles and the hidden psychic folds of her soul. Bodies were hidden about as well as a gas station in a wheat field in their dramatically optimal spots throughout the camp. A small, simple, bob-headed waif cornered in her sights getting in a lucky shot with her own damned machete.

The world spun until she realized she was the one spinning. Not even her. The majority of her slumping stubbornly to the ground, while the her that mattered flipped end over end before landing, useless, in the mud. There was a momentary hope that the horror, the trauma, and the constant rage would fade with condensing pupils, but no. No such mercy could exist in the face of so much ending.

Instead, there was the sitting. The waiting. The being scooped up and thrown into black bags that sealed away the light.

Movement. The return of the red rage. The inability to do anything with it. Memories of picnics and hope and fear and grief and anger in endless loops. Then, the miracle happened.

His face.

He had grown. Amid the moss and overgrown roots and whatever else lay at the bottom of the lake. Maybe her mind had lied and those last moments were an illusion, or he loved her too much to stop being.

It didn't matter that she couldn't see his face through the burlap sack. She knew his slow, patient gait. The angle of his head. The way of his silence, She knew her baby boy. She *felt* him.

He'd found her, filed away like old papers, and taken her to his home. He'd surrounded her with candles, so that she would never know the dark again. Brought her trinkets and the twisted faces of others like the ones who'd allowed his death and, therefore, caused hers.

Her pride and love swelled, filling him with what could not fit in the confines of her head, until that bitch stole her mirror and tricked him. She'd slammed sharpened metal through his collarbone and left him for dead with his mother's voice whispering betrayal into his ears.

Even when her own flesh had found her. When the hands lifting her from her cradle of cold, forgotten wax and stone were of grave dirt covered skin and bones that belonged to none other than herself. Even then, she couldn't bring herself to run to his arms.

In the shadows, she helped with whatever drew him along his path. Even when she failed to notice the empty middle blue mockery of his own central and split visceral red. She slid through the hidden background, cutting down those who sought to do him harm. She herself became his shadow.

In the background, through the lies of the woman or the bald child and in the echoes of lightning and even in the hideous slug crawling from mouth to mouth. She was there. Always there, building her own unnoticed body count. Even into the cold gulfs between the stars and onto a strange ball with wholly new shapes among the bright dots in the sky.

Silencing voices that would cause him harm.

With less bulk than his impressive frame. Less raw anger. More despair. More understanding of where this all leads. She'd hold a thousand weeping frames shuddering their last as long as the hope held that one day he would see her in the distance, hear her whispers of *mama cares*, and understand.

    Just once.

Jesus of Jim Beam

I'm just a monkey.

Here to dance for these stupid fuckers and their brainless goddamn amusement. Then they ship me off in my tidy little box. I've obliged more times than I want to count.

And I have to start again when I step out on this shitty stage of this shitty club filled with shitty people.

So I kick back a solid drag from my trusty handle of Jim Beam and take one last look in the scored-up aluminum sheet pretending to be a mirror. Have a quick think on my dumbass ideals and how much I used to believe fervently that I was gonna change the whole fucking thing.

Time to make Rock N Roll dangerous again. It's a fucking joke. I'm a fucking joke.

The house lights are out. Three Kleigs lined up in the center of the tiny corner stage are making me sweat already. The crowd is silent. They want to see what the monkey will do first.

Will he strip off his ratty drawers and squat on the stage? I heard he did that in Ontario. Maybe he'll just shit into the mouth of someone up front like he did in Cincinnati. Who will he punch? Who will he fuck? What will he insert? Where?

They don't notice that the band has started to play. They never do. Even though these guys have put everything they can into it. Have followed my dictum down to the letter. Harley's beating back on the father that beat him. Al's strangling the mother that left him gasping for air and screaming for food in a dumpster five minutes after his birth. Ian's running a knife across the throat of that dealer who got his sister hooked on ice and running her ass out on Santa Monica Boulevard. They fucking play it and they fucking mean it and these fuckers don't even care.

I go ahead and hold up the handle, chugging half the liter while I flip them off. It's probably the only part that isn't for show. I just want it over and I'd rather not remember it, if I could.

Then, I see him. Right up front. He's wearing a Lime polo and a big ass smile beaming up at me. It all hits me like a freight train.

Those years trying to make something real. Trying to be a bigger monster than they thought could exist and finding the same damn thing in every town. Stupid fucking privileged kids trying to piss their parents off, but not enough to lose the keys to the car. Mini-skirted skanks screaming for my cock, then screaming to daddy when I gave it to them right on the stage. All those frat and football motherfuckers like this asshole who didn't even know why they were here.

Fuck it.

I don't even wait for my cue. That chugging three bars that mean it's time for the usual banal hell to rain down. I just run straight for him and ram the microphone into those pearly white teeth. I can feel the impact. Feel them shatter. But I don't stop. I grab the back of his head and keep thrusting the mic like I'm trying to fuck his face with it. I keep forcing it until the teeth are nothing but ragged shards and I can push it past his torn and bleeding gums. Blood is pouring around the mic as I cram it into the back of his throat. Then I grab the cord and start to wrap it around his neck. I'm not sure if his eyes are bulging because of the pressure or from the surprise. This wasn't on the program. Eventually, his eyes roll up into his head and close. He goes limp. I know he's dead.

This is when the story is supposed to end. Some brave, tough as nails motherfucker stands up and beats me to death with my own mic stand. Or the whole crowd rushes me, including my own band. They hold me down and wait for the cops to arrive. I stare blankly at the judge that issues the demand for my execution. I bow my head and thank the person that flips the switch. Millions of electrons flood my body and this waste of time and effort will be over. Finally.

But it doesn't. Everyone screams for more. The next song is starting, even though I haven't sung a word. It's not the first time I was too drunk or stoned or pilled into the ground to bother doing my part. They still think it's all part of the show.

So I grab the girl standing next to his limp corpse. Maybe she thinks she's the lucky one. The one that gets to taste my dick before it's been covered in blood and shit. The cooze even winks at me. She starts to lower herself onto her knees and I oblige, but the only thing she tastes is the cheap wooden corner of the stage.

I pull her head back and scream skyward. Blood is running down her chin and she finally starts to fight back. Kicking at my shins. Clawing at the hand laced into her hair. It isn't enough. I put all of my force into it and slam her into the corner again. She goes limp. She may not be dead, but she'll still never wink like that again. I leave her where she lays and move on to the next person.

He's dancing. Can you believe that? Dancing. Through all of this. His head is shaved, so I can't grab him by the hair. So I hit him in the face with an elbow and he drops like a sack of apples. I drop too. My knee lands directly on his forehead and I feel the skull crunch. I continue dropping myself down on it. Shards of skull are tearing apart the skin on my knee and the pulped mush of his brains are leaking all over my leg. I remember hearing somewhere that brains have the highest count of bacteria compared to any other body part and get worried about infection for a moment. Then I remember all the things I have had on or inside me and laugh. It's the first time I have honestly, completely laughed in decades.

Now, people are finally starting to stare. The music's still going but the rhythm is off. Maybe Harley, Al, and Ian finally noticed that something real is happening for once. Or maybe they actually suck as bad as everyone says and I've never noticed till now.

I take advantage of their shock and grab the nearest guy within reach. As I'm shoving my thumbs into his eyes, I notice that he has "waste" tattooed on his forehead. True fact, but why advertise it? The thin bone behind the eyes is harder to break through than I assumed it would be. Still, he doesn't put up any fight and falls to the floor quickly. I grab off a girl's glasses and stab her in the throat with them. Three times. One guy, I simply knee in the crotch until he collapses.

I'm pretty sure my elbow is hitting someone in the back of the head while I punch some black-T sheep to death. Another's ribs give in when I jump on them twice. My boots sink three inches or so into him. That's when I notice the fist swinging in from the right.

I used to sit in malls, staring at the crowds of people lined up to buy more crap no one ever needs, and wonder how many people I could kill with my bare hands before anyone even tried to stop me. It felt nice to know the answer.

Seven.

I take the hit to the jaw and marvel at lights sparkling inside my head. It's been a while since anyone hit me that hard. I thank him by rushing into his chest. He hits the ground hard enough that I think his neck is broken.

Someone kicks me in the back. A cheap move, but I respect it. I turn around and twist his leg until the bone is sticking out of his flesh and leave him crying into the darkness.

A bottle hits me with a dull explosion of pain in the back of my neck. It hurts, but doesn't do any real damage. If you are going to go for the sneaky shot, you should make sure it counts. I grab the bottle out of his hand and break it on his neighbor's head. The poor slob falls to the floor and starts jigging like it's polka time. Then I stab the fucker who missed the sweet spot right in his jugular. To be sure the job is done right, I twist the bottle a couple times. He won't be going home tonight.

The game has become boring already. The same thing over and over again. A few more bodies fall to the ground. Dead or alive, it doesn't matter. The crowd has thinned out a bit. Some are probably running for the doors and the rest are backing off but still gawking like idiots.

I notice a big bull of a motherfucker wearing a "God Hates Fags" shirt. I almost respect the balls, but I want to have some fun. I rush in and hit him across the eyes with the broken bottle. Unsurprisingly, he squeals like a little girl. The big ones never know how to deal with someone coming at them.

I jump and headbutt him squarely in the forehead. When I land, I grab ahold of his nuts and squeeze. It feels like at least one of them bursts under the pressure and his legs give out. I step behind him and yank his pants to the ground. They're a bit tight, so he loses some skin in the process. With him face down on his knees and pants on the ground in front of me, I reach into my pants and pull out my cock. Leaving him with the memory that he's been fucked in the ass in front of the few people that remain amuses me more than killing him.

It leaves me vulnerable. Someone will make their move to take me out. I'm sure of it, but don't let it stop me. I thrust into his ass with no lubrication, letting the blood that wells up from the torn tender skin do the work. The sensation of my two balls flapping into his one remainder is strange but not unpleasant. I'm sure I manage to work at him for a full minute at least before I cum and leave him to wilt on the floor.

Still, no one has moved to stop me.

Twenty or so featureless faces surround me. Someone somewhere half-heartedly yells "Life Sucks, Scum Fuck" and I think about the stories they might have to tell. Will they be full of terror and excitement? Will blood pound in the ears of the listener? Or will it be more pointless tales of minor accomplishments at work? Another day and thousands more breaths wasted on nothing whatsoever.

On the Frustrations of Modern Wendigos

Enough time in the woods, wandering lost and alone and desperate to the point of gnawing on thistles in the hope that somewhere between bitter jabs might rest some illusion of a nutrient, and anyone would chew the neck out of their best friend.

"Wasn't that Thoreau? Seems like something he would've said during that fool-ass self-isolation binge. Another excuse to chase himself away."

It is all natural enough. This call of flesh. The acids in your stomach yearn to pry apart chemical bonds to find the microscopic explosions hidden so well within them. The once-sharp edges of your teeth need skin and sinew and muscle. They desire the opportunity to force themselves between nested folds of compressed protein with the same desperation as your lungs craving to be filled to bursting with the miniscule exhalations of vegetation. It is just what you are.

"Yeah. I get it. Red. Tooth. Claw. Yattah Yattah. But have you considered the idea that now may not be the time to lean on the whole 'natural' thing? I've had just about as much nature as I can fucking handle. I'm not much interested in more of it. A chemical-rich, near plastic puff pastry from the back aisles of the shittiest quickstop in the county would do me just fine right now."

You are responding to the conditioning of the city. The strictures of those concrete structures have built up their lattice along the lining of your skull. Caged your spirit in angular prisms, shifting and splitting the light, scattering photons so that they but brush barely against your true being. Starving it of truth until the lies of that artificial existence seem the only possible path.

"Funny point you decided to rest on there. That whole starving of the spirit bit. As if I'm not physically fucking starving right goddamn now. And do you know what is starving me? Come on, dearest disembodied voice in my head. You know the answer to this pop quiz, hotshot. That paragon of industrialization, with its unnatural splatters of assembly line burger and bun beneath the fabled golden arches never left me high, dry, and near dead quite like dear old mother nature is doing right now."

Then think instead of that craving in your pit. Let images of skull skin, peeled back like the rind of an overripe fruit, fill your mind. The wormy, spongy grey meat that lays just beneath a thin shell of bone, pulsing with dreams and memories and spare, desperate yearnings that can never be quite spoken. The sweetbreads that are neither sweet, nor bread but fill the mind almost more than the belly. Think on what kidneys, pierced, spitted, and still dripping hot blood onto the coals of a fresh fire, smell like as their skin crackles in the heat. Let the saliva filling your mouth marinate on that.

"Yeah. Starting with brains and kidneys is a great motivator you landed on there. Always my first and second pick from the value menu, those two. Nothing quite gets the tum-tum rumbling like ruminating on Kuru or munching on piss-organs. Yeah, I know what's in sausage. Chorizo is my shit despite being mostly lymph glands and jalapenos and I abso-fucking-lutely love it but I doubt you have a grinder, let alone a fully stocked spice rack out here. I mean, that may have been fennel a little while back or it may have just been some other plant with, like, seeds on it. I wouldn't goddamn know the difference."

That disconnection you feel is what loses-

"Not to mention the whole problem with the fire you so casually mentioned. I can barely get those pressed-sawdust logs from the grocery store to light up with the aid of a half-gallon of gasoline. How in the ever-loving asscrack of apathetic existence do you actually believe that I could manage to conjure flames from damp, fallen, green wood without even so much as a book of bar matches?"

The answer to this lost past lies just within the flesh of those you once called your brethren-

"And that's another thing. You put waaaaaaaay too much trust in my ability to access that much vaunted flesh. Just a couple of days ago, I saw what had to be the world's most injured raccoon. Dragging its hind legs through the dirt like two sticks tied loosely to its back and bleeding like a blown hose. Still couldn't catch that damn thing. Got near enough for it to turn into a blur of nails, teeth, and piercing, raging noise. And that almost dead rodent was the one to get a meal out of the deal, scurry-pulling its way through the underbrush with a good half-finger gripped in its mouth."

But if you would only heed the call-

"So what am I supposed to do? Sharpen some stick that fell out of a tree, since I'm pretty sure the keys to an old Camry won't saw their way through a branch? Watch it shatter when I try to sink it into the skin of an unwary hiker with even less sense than me before they stomp my malnourished ass into the dirt? Do my best to claw my way through their skin with these split, ragged nails-"

WILL YOU JUST SHUT THE FUCK UP FOR A FUCKING MINUTE?!

Seriously. Two weeks and all you've done is carp and whine about how you just can't pull it off and I've done my bit. I've slithered in with the wind. Poisoned your hope. Stoked your hunger. But if I have to deal with one more self-defeating, self-important syllable of whining nonsense then I will find a way to materialize corporally and beat you with your own fucking foot.

"Um-"

Shhh, now. Poppa's talking here, kiddo. What if I told you that just about a mile north of here there is a campsite?

"How-"

Yes, I know you can't find north from the inside of your own ass. I'll show you. Stop fucking whinging and fucking listen.

What if there was a lone campsite with a lone camper, his fire still burning far brighter than he should have left it as he drifted off? What if he was already out of the running due to the half bottle of Old Number Seven thinning his blood and pulling his brain from its body? What if I told you that you couldn't find an easier corpse to gnaw on?

"Wait. There's whiskey?"

Beautiful Things

"Why the hell are you doing this, Frank?" Tim asked. Five minutes outside and the sweat was already running rivers down his face, filling in the crevices and cracks that line his eyes and mouth. If anyone thought to ask, he'd have given just about anything to get back into the house where there was at least some shade. Anything but this. "You know he's gone. Been this long… one way or another, he's out of your reach. You *know* that."

"Don't know what you're talking about, Timmy, old boy," Frank said, with a smile that didn't completely touch his lips, let alone reach his eyes. Unable to meet his old friend's gaze, he focused on his fifth cataloging of items in his backpack. "I'm just going to do some reconnaissance. See how far out I can get from here before running into too many of the bastards. Pick up some extra supplies if possible. Maybe meet up with another group like ourselves. "

"Don't 'Timmy Old Boy' me and don't for a second think I'm

falling for your bullshit. He did a damn fool thing and now you want to feed yourself to whatever stinking, shambling piece of shit happens to stumble across you out there because of it? I'm telling you, let him go."

"I can't," Frank said, "He's my son, dammit. The only job I have, the only one that ever mattered, is to look after him and I failed. I failed him. I failed whatever is left of the memory of his mother and I failed the most basic functions of nature. I fucking failed," Frank's voice finally cracked, eyes filled with more water than seemed possible. Great gleaming lakes teeming with anger, guilt, and fear threatened to break and drown the world.

Tim didn't bother responding. Instead, he relaxed, waiting for the silence to fill itself in. Sometimes you had to let a man have his say, get it out of his system, and then hope he would listen to reason.

"Did I ever tell you about the night I finally decided to leave the house?"

"Yep. Wife dead, then not. Growl. Moan. Bite. Screams, crying, and eventually a crushed skull later convincing you that it was time to take the kid for a road trip. I don't want to sound calloused, but we've all told our tales enough that I could recite everyone's verbatim."

"I didn't tell you everything."

The only thing Frank could feel was a numb throbbing in his foot. Everything had taken on a cloudy haze, like he was living in a Lifetime movie of the week. His heart was beating far too fast. His head was pounding. The house was dead quiet but there was too much internal noise for him to focus. A muffled thump at his right caught his attention and, after what seemed like a Herculean struggle against the independent will of the muscles controlling his eyes and neck, he noticed a malformed lump shining dimly in the scant light.

Whatever it was, it was squat, lumpy, and of a shape that vaguely suggested some long lost intention of roundness. The irregular turquoise gloss, bare clay randomly showing through like bits of exposed bone, caught the light filtering in through the slats in the boarded up window.

Finally, something his mind could wrap itself around: a present from Johnny, a school project from earlier this year when the schools were still open. But he didn't remember the bottom of it being so dark, almost black. Mind still too fuzzy, too empty to be sure.

He could remember the first time he had seen it: a mutated aberration as heavy as a Volvo and just about as ugly. Then there was Johnny's face, twisted up in a mixture of anger and shame bespeaking the end of all that is good and pure in existence. The boy had wanted to destroy it on the sidewalk right there, though Frank was pretty sure it would have done more damage to the concrete than vice versa. In swooped Eileen, stern face carved in granite, sharply demanding that he do no such thing before settling into a dissertation on abstract art and the importance of imperfection as the highest form of beauty. Any mother could placate a sad child with smothering hugs and sloppy kisses, but nobody could commit to a line of bullshit like she could and Johnny fell for it whole-heartedly.

On her next birthday, it held a place of honor in the middle of the dining room table.

Now that table was in pieces around the room and as much as he needed to get up off the floor, he couldn't. Couldn't pick himself up. Couldn't move. What good would it do?

Everything was falling apart out there. The repeated assurances that, as long as everyone remained in their homes, the authorities would sort it all out weren't worth the gas they were propelled on. He'd always laughed at the unwashed, dreadlocked buffoons that constantly circled the Plant screaming about the end of humanity's reign on earth, but it looks like they were right all along.

When he had come down to investigate the moans, he was struck by the raw, gamey stench that rolled in waves from the dining room/kitchen combo at the back of the house. None of them had bathed for far too long, but only an idiot and a dead man could mistake sweat and dirt for the slaughterhouse reek of fresh spilled blood. Running into the room, he almost slipped ass over teakettle in the thick crimson pool on linoleum that had always been a bitch to keep white and never would be so again. His immediate thought was that one of them had broken in, that the boards and scrap wood scavenged from furniture had been no match for the patience of something with nothing else to lose. He had to get Eileen and Johnny the hell out of there before more caught on and their sanctuary became a sepulcher.

Then he noticed the writing on the wall.

These things were sloppy eaters, there was no arguing that, but he had never known one to take the time to write 'sorry for the mess' in blood before. He recognized the ragged haircut on the groaning monstrosity that had started shuffling toward him even though the hair was the wrong color, no longer the shining gold that always caught the morning sun in its own gleaming furnace. Just yesterday, he had managed to convince her to get rid of those long, flowing locks that hadn't seen a pair of scissors since she was a little girl. She finally agreed that it made far too easy of a handhold and they had all seen too many times what happened once one of them grabbed you.

With the thought of that deadly grip in his mind and time compressing around him as if the world was suddenly trapped in drying amber, he noticed that its hands and fingers hung loosely on its wrists. Old Universal Mummy limpness, instead of the usual rigid claws, drawing attention to the torn flesh running from the inside of the wrists up to the elbows of both arms. Even though nothing had managed to breach their defenses, death had wormed its way into the house.

Suddenly as a tiger pouncing from among the high sugar

cane, the flow of time returned to normal and the luxury of rational thought was beyond him. Running on instinct alone, he grabbed the nearest sturdy object and began pounding. Untrained, undisciplined, no style or form whatsoever. A flurry of fear and rage that was over before he truly understood what was happening.

That had to have been hours ago; long enough for the sun to start its morning crawl over a lost world. Half the night spent standing in the same spot, staring emptily at anything except the mess on the floor directly beneath him. He wasn't sure if he'd been crying or if it was just blood drying on his face, but he knew there was a choice being made here. Perhaps it already had been. He took one last look down at the piece of Avant Garde and went to get his son.

It was time to get the fuck out of Dodge.

"I know it's a cliché, but then let it be a fucking cliché. He was the only reason I bothered to move from that spot," Frank said. "She had been unfailingly upbeat, constantly telling us it would all be over soon and we'd be able to move on with our lives, but she just couldn't fool herself anymore. That was what cut it for me, what tore the survival instinct right out of my heart: if the queen bullshitter couldn't believe her own lines anymore then there really wasn't any hope left. Better to sit there and starve, or even be eaten, than waste yourself fighting what couldn't be fought. I was done.

"But that ugly ass hunk of clay reminded me that I wasn't alone in this. *I* may not have seen any reason to continue, but I didn't have the right to make that decision for *him*. I had to at least try to keep him alive long enough for him to decide his own fate and that's the only reason I'm here today. I owe him my life."

"There are people here that need you, too," Tim said. "Just as much as he did then."

"My ass they do. Never would've made it here in the first place if they didn't know how to take care of themselves. They'll be fine."

"OK. We both know better than this stupidity, but there's no convincing a fool when he's determined. You understand that the only way we're likely to see you again is limping, moaning, and smelling like year old Limburger left to ripen in the back of a Pacer in August, right?"

"Yep."

"Then I won't stand in your way. But you're going to wait an extra day and I won't hear any arguing against it. There's no way in hell I'm going to let you leave me alone with those whippersnappers."

***

They were working their way down the freeway when they heard the first one moaning. Pretty pathetic display, even for a dead man, but it was enough to put them on guard. With no sightings, Tim and Frank became more paranoid each day. In some ways, they were a bit relieved to hear one simply because the sound let them know where it was.

They held back and waited on top of what once may have been a lime green Ford Escape. Neither of them quite liked being so exposed, but at least the highway offered plenty of obstacles to slow down any attackers. Guard rails on the sides would have to be clambered over and the cars piled into and over each other every foot or so provided few paths and set up marvelous choke points. As long as they didn't run into any large hoards, it was workable.

A hundred yards off, he saw them coming. Five. Mobile in their own way, but pretty far gone: not a single hair to split between them, flesh sloughing off in greasy chunks as they squeezed between rusting, jutting pieces of metal. One that Frank certainly hoped had been a woman back when it mattered still wore a moldering, yet screaming red vinyl skirt that cut into the meat of her stomach and legs as she slouched along.

"Would you look at that," Tim exclaimed, pointing out an enormous hulk of a former human being. "I do believe he has a good bit of his large intestine hanging out of his ass. Gonna need himself a hemorrhoid donut."

Worrying about silence once those things started calling out was pointless. Once some started in, any others within range to hear it would follow. At that point, being quiet was just an exercise in stubbornness.

Frank didn't say anything.

Both of them unshouldered a bludgeon. Tim slowly swung the Morningstar they'd found in an abandoned storefront and Frank's simple but reliable crowbar hung lazily by his side.

And they waited.

And waited.

And waited.

Until the first one, the one with a ragged stump of shit-snake hanging out of its ample ass, finally waddled into range.

"I guess it'll be age before beauty," Tim said, dramatically gesturing toward the maggot meals-on-wheels tank.

Swinging in a wide arc, he landed a well-practiced hit into its temple and the results went well beyond his expectations. The grapefruit sized ball hit with enough force to cave in half of the thing's skull and the spikes slid in like butter. The beast slumped to the ground.

Frank, impressed as he was with Tim's skull-o-matic, opted for the straightforward approach with the tart in red vinyl. As she began to claw and scrape at the side of the vehicle, bits of bone and flesh tumbling beneath her, he shoved the point of Ol' Reliable into her eye socket. With a squelch and a pop, it broke through the thin bone behind the eye cavity and punctured the brain, taking the little light that remained out of her other eye.

When someone has done the same thing enough times, their muscles begin to know what to do before they have the opportunity to consciously think about it. The body acts on its own, doing as it has been trained, and too much interference from the brain only gets in the way. One good side effect is that this allows the mind to wander off to ponder any subject it wished. A negative side effect is that the mind tends to enjoy focusing on the things that do the most damage.

"Take a deep breath...Line up your shot. Breathe out slowly and fire," Frank said, shaking much more than Johnny was.

He couldn't help being nervous dragging his son out here among the lost. The roof was clear and the building was long enough to make it highly unlikely that any of them would crowd the back fire escape. As long as they moved quickly once the swarming started, they should be able to miss out on any serious concentration. He'd taken worse risks with Tim and even some of the other youngsters out on scavenging raids without the slightest worry, but he couldn't get past the fact that this was his son and he was putting him in danger. If something went wrong, if they had misjudged anything at all, and Johnny died out here today, he would have no one to blame but himself.

At the same time, he knew that this was necessary. The days where a man could coddle and spoil his child were long gone. Living forever had never been an option and his chances of making it back seemed to get slimmer each time he left the two-floor, one acre compound they called home. Taking him out into this might possibly kill him, but hiding him behind those walls would definitely do it just as surely as if he had ripped his son's steaming guts out himself. The boy needed to know how to survive on his own out here and training on a dummy could only take him so far. Frank knew well enough the difference between shooting paper targets and taking aim at a wailing, flailing, biting mass of rotted flesh that was once a regular human being. Worse was feeling the throbbing pain pulse up to your shoulder and the wet splatter of old blood and congealed putrescence across your face as you smash a brainpan up close.

"Holy fuck!" Johnny shouted after nailing one directly between the eyes. "Did you see that? I swear that splatter looks just like a butterfly's wing." He giggled just a little before lining up the next one.

Frank was a little surprised by how quickly and easily Johnny was taking to his work. He didn't flinch at the violence or hesitate with any of the worry about the monster's former humanity that had so plagued Frank early on. He also didn't seem to possess any of the malice or hatred that often arose as a way to combat the inevitable guilt. They were just things that needed to be destroyed.

He almost envied his son for having grown up in this world. The boy would never get to see a game at The Great American Ballpark or marvel at how tiny everything looked from the window of an airplane. He wouldn't have the opportunity to know the feeling of true and complete safety. He wouldn't even get to endure the embarrassment of dancing with his mother at his wedding. But he would never be held back from doing what survival dictated by memories of the way the world once was.

"Lori keeps going on and on about Jackson Pollock paintings," Johnny said while reloading, now having to shout over the growing din of the moaning multitudes below. "I wonder what she'd think of the patterns I'm making."

Watching his son perfectly comfortable in his work, Frank

felt a level of pride that disturbed and calmed him. He knew that his time as mentor, coach, and father was nearing an end. He also knew his son would be fine.

***

"Shit, Frank," Tim said, trying his best to keep from meeting his friend's blank stare. "I don't know what the hell to say. I told you this was a damn fool thing to do."

Frank didn't bother to respond. Wasn't sure he could even if he wanted to. Couldn't breathe, couldn't think straight from the shock. He had finally come to his own personal Armageddon.

They'd been following the signs for about two weeks since their first sighting on the highway. A simple name, destination, and date spray-painted directly on the asphalt every mile or so. It was something they had worked out for scavenging runs, a demand drilled into everyone's skulls. The idea was to allow for the possibility of rescue in case of injury or becoming surrounded, giving a search party a regular update on location and travel time. Seeing Johnny's name was a two-fold relief to Frank, not only reassuring him that his son had at least made it this far but also that he was still thinking, despite his temper tantrum. Maybe it meant that he actually wanted his father to come after him. He wanted to come home and stop acting like a jackass.

For some idiot reason, Johnny had gone into the city. The first place everyone with any sense left. A high population crammed into close quarters meant a quick and easy spread, like ripples through a lake. Even if the local hoards had migrated to somewhere else in search of food, there were still the blockades to deal with. Worthless walls, thrown together during the early stages to block off the street, made of whatever crap could be found in the nearby buildings: old mattresses and bed frames, bookshelves, ovens, washing machines, tables, etc. Not only was there no way in hell such a slapdash job could work, but now the materials were mostly rotten or rusted and they posed nearly as much of a risk as the occasional creepy crawly still trapped within.

After squeezing their way through one of these death traps, Frank and Tim had noticed a pulped mass of putrid flesh on the concrete. What they could only guess had once been a human had been utterly destroyed. Bones hadn't just been shattered, but pulverized and what meat remained had been beaten into a thick soup. This wasn't the typical M.O. for a flesh-hungry beast, only your garden variety human was capable of this kind of savagery.

That was when they saw him.

The hair was what clinched it. Who else would wear the long, tightly bound braid of a Chinese monk from the cheesy kung-fu flicks they had watched together so often? Certainly no one else with the delicate blond he somehow managed to get from his mother, glimmers of gold shining through the dirt and grime it had amassed.

Not having sensed their presence yet, he simply stood there. Still, relaxed, probably the calmest Frank had ever seen him. He looked malnourished. Bones jutted at every angle under pallid skin. He was missing his right hand from the wrist down. Jagged threads of skin and sinew dangled like tinsel from the nubs of bone.

Tim knew what had to be done. No father should have to do this shit, even though they all had. He unslung a dented and crusted aluminum baseball bat, the Morningstar having proved a tad too unwieldy to be practical, and walked towards *it*.

Until he felt a grip as solid as granite on his shoulder.

"I can't let you do that, Tim," Frank said to him as he turned around, locking his gaze with eyes that practically blazed with regret and resolution. He should have known it was going to go this way.

Frank had been on his way to relieve Johnny of the much despised night watch a couple hours early. He couldn't sleep and, after the fight that afternoon, he hoped maybe it would calm the boy down a bit. Besides, they hadn't heard a single moan or scrape for months so it wasn't going to be a particularly stressful watch.

This lack of recent contact was precisely what had started the argument earlier in the day. Johnny was certain that any real threat was over and that it was time to start long-range scouting expeditions in hope of finding other survivors. He wasn't the only one, but everyone else had agreed to wait through the next winter freeze and spring thaw since those processes would speed up decomposition of any remainders out there. Their compound was completely self-sufficient thanks to the supreme luck of a working well and a garden fertilized by their new waste disposal techniques. There was no reason to push their luck and risk any more than they had to, but Johnny wouldn't hear it. If they continued to wait, they could be damning another group of holdouts to starvation. They were being selfish, he said.

Frank immediately saw this for the con it was. Johnny felt cooped up. He wanted to get out and meet new people. Mostly, he was horny. He seemed to honestly believe that he would ride into another compound on a glittering white horse to thunderous applause and accolades from women simply dying to get a hold of his cock.

So there had been a fight, with all of the petulance and anger that accompanies any argument with a teenager. Where logic and reason had failed, demands had been laid out in the face of grumbling and pouting and you-don't-understands. He'd spent the night locked in his room, but at least went out on watch peaceably enough.

As Frank began a perimeter walk along the wall, he heard the earnest whispers that could only mean another argument. It came as no surprise to anyone that the teens were the first ones to adapt a form of whisper that conveyed the tone and intent of top-of-the lungs, throat shredding screams. Determined to keep his distance, he stuck to the shadows as he checked out the situation.

As it turned out, Johnny was in a bit of a spat with Lori, the only girl in the compound near his age. When they hit puberty, there had been plenty of speculation about the possibility of a relationship between them, but nothing developed.

"Come on Lori," Johnny insisted, "I just want a kiss. Just for good luck."

"You're so full of shit, J," Lori spit back. "We both know you wouldn't want to stop there. I've told you over and over again: I. AM. NOT. INTERESTED. So keep your dick in your pants."

There was no question in Frank's head about what was going on here, but he didn't step in. Sometimes a boy needed to be shot down. What he didn't need was to know that he was being shot down right in front of his old man. Still, boys have been known to do stupid things in these moments, so he wasn't going anywhere.

"Why do you have to be such a bitch about this?" Johnny said, pressing in on Lori's personal space. She was obviously

uncomfortable, but holding her ground. There was no room left for any damsels in distress in the world and she had earned her bad-ass wings out there just like everyone else. "I'm the one who always risked his ass while you got to jaunt around on your little shopping sprees. Don't you think you owe me a little?"

That was when he decided to pounce, pushing her to the ground, and throwing himself on top of her. Frank couldn't believe that Johnny was actually stupid enough, asshole enough, to try something like this. He couldn't let this continue.

But before he could do anything, Lori slammed her elbow into Johnny's nose, breaking it. Taking advantage of his momentary pain and confusion, she pushed herself out from under him and stood up.

"I don't owe you a damn thing," she growled. "I've done my fair share, just like everyone else. Hell, I've killed more of them close up than you have from the safety of your little rooftops. If you ever touch me again, I'll use your nuts to flavor our next soup." After kicking him in the side twice to hammer the point in, she stomped off back toward the house.

Frank didn't know what to do or how to deal with the

situation. Behavior like this couldn't stand, but now didn't seem like the time to address it. For the moment, Johnny wasn't going to be doing anything and a lecture wouldn't have nearly the impact as that broken nose. He decided to slink his way back to the house and spend the night considering what to do in the morning. Maybe, given time to think about it, Johnny would realize what he had done and apologize on his own. In the meantime, Frank would leave his son with whatever little dignity he retained.

By morning, Johnny was nowhere to be found. The house was alive with the groanings and mumblings of its residents. He had left no note, no explanation, and not much food. The shit had taken about a quarter of it with him on his temper tantrum and he didn't bother to close the damn gate on his way out.

It was time to go through the whole hackneyed bit. Wasting time they didn't have, explaining something both of them already knew. It was pure fucking stupidity, but Tim went ahead with it anyways. What else were friends for?

"Frank, he's not your boy anymore."

"*Tim,*" Frank responded, the fury in his eyes dying down to the rough glaze of poorly fired pottery, "he hasn't been my boy for a long time."

The reassuring weight of Ol' Reliable firmly in hand, Frank walked over to meet his son.

She Stalks These Streets as Her Own Forest

Here, eyes glow, reflecting the electric neon that pulses with the whine of static from melted sand tubes and copper conductors that festoon the concrete structures. The quality isn't the same as she is used to. No soft, plaid glow condensed from moonlight shining out from twinned tapetum lucidum filtered through shifting leaves. This is harsher, more aggressive. Predatory.

Hers are no different. So they go unnoticed in the glare and flickers from so many beckoning tubes and bulbs. They don't notice much, she realizes. There are too many things to grab the eyes. Too many hands reaching out and yanking them this way and that. No wonder the wolves and bears and others defined by teeth and hunger slide in among them without so much as a whimper of warning.

Rough concrete scrapes against her feet. The bare flesh sloughing off in noticed severance, so unusual compared to the harsh clash of hoof to stone. Yet she bears it, a new pain to hold her tighter to this new hunt. As the trees wither and those who held to them move away, so must she. She has her place in the universe and must keep to it.

"Hey, bitch," a voice calls out from the noisy dark, "Why don't you give us a little smile? Bet you are prettier when you smile."

Her muscles tense, thighs and calves tight. Ready to leap. Tendons on the over and underside of digits she always has to readjust to contract and relax in alternating undulation. These alien anatomies connect in hidden neural pathways, but they take time to access. She relaxes her breathing. Remembers the forest, the flow of the wind through the leaves, and moves her lungs in concert with the memory.

This isn't the time to flee. Hiding among the branches and underbrush isn't an option here. Besides, she is here for a reason.

The blood called her.

Running isn't an option.

Neither is hiding. Those aren't her purpose. It's in the hunt, twisted back on the hunter. The prey turned predator. She knows this deep down past the doe-bound instinct.

She turns to the shadows, sniffing subtly. Flared nostrils

would alert the prey and let it know of the shift in dynamic, so she concentrates on the softness of her breath. Keeps it slow and deep and her eyes wide, as if the light pouring from them is just a reflection of the wonder around her. She shifts her head just slightly toward the call.

"Yeah, baby, " he yells. She can smell the acrid alcohol on his breath, sharp even amid the smoke and rot of the city. It reeks of a desperation she knows he would never name. "You know I'm talkin' to you. Give daddy a peek at the teeth between those sweet lips, sweetie."

There's a shudder between the words, a vulnerability underneath the bravado. The herd is watching. The other bulls. He knows it. He fears it.

This is the point of shifting where he turns ugly and the claws and teeth bare themselves. She doesn't need the history or even to smell the blood that has soaked into his skin to know where it could lead. Too many moons have cycled for her innocence to withstand such things.

So she turns, slightly shifting of angle and light in the unnatural neon glow. Enough for him to see the upward tilt of lips and reinforce the confidence he knows is his by right.

Just the right switch to the sway of her hips is enough to set the hook. She knows he is hers. Without a look back she knows he is following her away from the herd. Down the drab shadows of an alley, so like the shadowed clefts into hidden dead ends of the mountains of her youth. Narrowed paths of escape set in for those who think themselves the hunter.

And he bites deeper. The hook sets in further. He follows her, certain of an easy meal to fill the gaping, endless need inside of him. She can almost taste the blood that has filled his mouth, and hear the exultant cries of seed he has sown in unwilling soil.

A look back is all it takes. Contact with his own empty orbs generating electricity of its own chemical sort. Then she can smell the shift in pheromones. She knows that he has claimed her as his. She can even see the responses in others, unconscious as it is. They shy away, acknowledging his claim.

Other females also move away, flowing in waves ever further distant. Understanding that a target has been planted, often at more of an instinctual level than intellectual. They know, without knowing, that a threat has been diverted and their own desires can be more reasonably directed now. Knowing, even without necessarily understanding, they move in on their own prey.

Still, he closes in. Certain of the kill and the accomplishment that will exalt him in the eyes of his fellows. He knows, without any doubt, that she belongs to him. Her own will matters little in such decisions.

She can sense his confidence as she sways her way down an alley. The path does not matter to her. She has found her way down such ways in the past without issue, some place separate from the pack. A way divorced from assistance.

In the dark of shadows, where the neon and sputtering unnatural light ceases to penetrate, she pauses.

"Come to me," she lets the words, slimy and moss-strewn as they are, slip from her lips. She feels a minute disgust at the simplicity and emptiness of the words and the ruse. She has her own needs to feed and she can taste the torn flesh and lives rended by this particular beast in the air surrounding him. Sometimes, fairness has already been surpassed before her own snares come into play and she understands her part in the greater weave. "I have worlds in my folds you have never seen."

When, in the morning, hoofprints and the ragged tears of antlers in flesh strewn over brick and macadam are taken apart and pieced back together, she hopes someone will see the blood still stuck in the teeth of those who feast on no flesh but that which they feel most accessible.

Blood In, Blood Out

Jim had known well enough, when he pulled into the drive-thru, that the "fast" part of fast food would apply just as much as the food part. Somewhere deep inside of him, there was a cold, rational voice asking politely for him to calm down and stop acting like a jackass but he was determined not to listen to the smug little fucker. Not today. Today, he couldn't care less who saw him flailing around inside his car, red face screaming as he beat on the steering wheel and not a damn person moving one goddamn, motherfucking, ass sucking, donkey punching, mother fisting, whale felating inch.

"Shit," he yelled out as he jerked the wheel to the right and pulled out of the line. He was still hungry and now he was running an extra five minutes late. Even though he knew it was his own fault for piddling around in the morning and staying up way too late the night before, he still railed at the pimpled wastes working the window for not bending the laws of physics and minimum wage for him.

He hated showing up late to class, it always played out the same way: The wheeze and whine of an unoiled door would draw every eye in the room to him. Then, the professor would lash out with some snarky comment as those eyes bored into him, following every step until he found the first available seat to slump into. Usually, that would leave him stuck at the front of the class instead of some nice, shadowed corner in the back, where he preferred to hide. Doing it on the first day would be worse. He might be made an example of, providing a nice laugh for everyone else in the room and marking him for the rest of the semester. The idea of embarrassment was almost enough to convince him to turn around and go back to bed, but school was the only reason he hadn't been booted from the house yet.

It's not like he didn't know any of this the night before when he was rereading and annotating a worn Lovecraft anthology into the wee hours of the night for the fifth time. No less so in the morning as he promptly plopped down on the couch to watch TV with a blanket pulled over his head. He knew better, but those voices from the outside helped fill up his head, pushing out the one that would inevitably rise up to echo off the forgotten walls. The voice full of questions without answers: low, dejected, and prodding for motion, for action, for *something* even though inertia dictated it would never happen.

His life was what it was, trapped between dry pages of dusty books and narratives played out in computer-crafted pixels, and it wasn't going to be changing any time soon.
This was exactly the type of situation his parents always brought up when pushing for him to move onto campus. After all, there were plenty of cheap places within ten minutes' walking distance of the school, some of them a damn sight nicer than the house he was living in. No more hour-long car trips to get to a class that only lasted 45 minutes and he wouldn't have to put his social life on hold for them. A good joke, that one. What dear old daddy and mummy really wanted was to stop putting *their* social life on hold for *him*, and he couldn't blame them. They had signed up for 18 years, not the 25 plus it was turning out to be. Still, the idea of calling some stranger and shacking up with them and four or five friends was repellant to him and there was no way he would be able to afford to live on his own.

So here he was, driving in circles around those same rented houses, looking for an open parking space while cursing at the top of his lungs. *These damn people don't even need cars.*

The least they can do is keep them off the street, he thought. After wasting another five minutes, he managed to wedge himself into something vaguely resembling a parking spot before throwing his bag over his shoulder and stepping out into the rain. Of course, it had to be raining! With at least a fifteen minute umbrella-less slog ahead of him, he put his head down and growled to himself. Finally, he made it to the relative dryness of the Friar Building and attacked the stairs like they were his own personal giants and windmills. Like the side entrance stairs in every college building to ever exist, they were tight and cramped with metal steps that clanged his name with each step. One advantage of being late was that he avoided the throngs of chattering dimwits who would choke this path to near impassibility. He double checked the crumpled class schedule to be sure he was going into the right room, took a deep breath, opened the door, and walked in.

"Mr. Wallstone, I assume?" said the man at the front of the room, presumably the professor. Jim was too busy searching for a chair to look at him. "There are copies of the syllabus on the table by the door. Please take one and have a seat."

"Um-hm," Jim responded, barely audible, head still bowed as he picked up the sizable packet. He didn't want to meet the staring, judging eyes that he knew must be locked onto him at this point, so he made for the first open desk he noticed.

Of course, it's in the middle of the room, the screeching voice in his head chimed in. *How else could I be the main act of this stupid fucking circus?*

Slouching into his chair, he began to vigorously scan the syllabus. Not reading or even seeing the words, his thoughts too scattered for that. It was only an excuse to keep from looking into any of the faces he was sure were turned his way, under the auspice of finding his place and catching up. It didn't stop him from feeling the eyes on him from everywhere in the room or hearing the intermittent giggles and grumbles, but it provided a focus so that he didn't have to acknowledge them.

Eventually, the class settled back into the established routine of feigned attention paid to the droning at the front of the room. The weight on his back lifted as those accusing faces turned forward or slumped onto hands strategically placed to give the impression of interest. The dull monotony of the lecture was a welcome reprieve, helping him smooth out his heart rate and calm the tumult of embarrassment in his mind.

He lifted his head, intending to glean something useful

from that featureless voice when a bit of purple caught his eye from a couple rows up. It was just an arm, attached to a person like any other. He knew he shouldn't be staring like this, that it was rude and would probably draw attention to him that he didn't want. He was being exactly the kind of douche nozzle he couldn't stand. Still, his eyes were locked in place.

    It *was* just an arm, though surely larger than average. Flabby, loose, and floppy. Oozing in lumps off the side of the desk, like cheap candle wax. Most of the skin was a nearly luminescent pale white, which accented the blotchy, mulberry stained underside. It was almost as if someone had half-filled white trash bags with Merlot. The appendage was further offset by his other arm and the rest of him, which was quite unremarkable. If not for that arm, the guy would have been the epitome of the generic college student: a white male in his late teens with a medium build, tousled hair, and slightly pasty skin. But it was there and it was consuming the man, overshadowing all of his other features in Jim's eyes.

    He felt horrible for staring the way he was. This guy was obviously suffering from some medical issue that bloated up his arm and caused the blood to pool in it. It had to be uncomfortable and finding shirts that fit such a lopsided frame couldn't be easy. The last thing he needed was some asshole gawking at him like the main attraction at a freak show.

Jim forced himself to concentrate on the front of the room where the professor was fidgeting with the SmartBoard while saying something about social paradigms and the psychological necessity of the Other. He had signed up for this class, Outcasts in Pop Culture, because it seemed like a cakewalk. No $120 textbook and most of the class time spent watching sitcoms and movies. If they were going to be using terms like that, then he might have made a horrid choice.

As this new fear was starting to creep its way along his spine, the professor turned around and, for a moment, he couldn't breathe. The elderly man's face was a complicated knot of scars, smooth lines crisscrossing over wrinkled cheeks and wrapping around an unnaturally cleft chin and spiraling out from his nose. Jim's first thought was that someone had worked at him with a weed whacker. The glassy, unmoving left eye spoke of damage beyond the superficial.

Stuck somewhere between pity and revulsion, it took every ounce of his resolve to hold down the reactions that threatened to bubble up from his throat. As much as he would've hated to admit it, his first thought was, *How do they expect me to learn anything from this guy?* He knew it was intolerant and a horrid thought to have, but it was there anyways. Without a doubt, he was finding himself completely unable to concentrate on the lesson at hand and he couldn't look at the man without following the lines, loops, and whorls of his scars.

He needed to look like he was paying attention, since profs tended to find an inattentive student more insulting than an actively disruptive one, but he couldn't keep looking at that face without something of his reaction showing up on his own visage. Insulting the man who holds his grades and loan status in his hands would be an academic death sentence. As it was, Jim hadn't made the best of impressions.

With no book to concentrate on and no paper to feign taking notes, he opted for looking near the guy instead of directly at him. It wasn't a perfect solution, and he was sure it looked a little odd, but he hoped it would work enough to get him through the day. He'd worry about the rest of the semester when he got there.

While his gaze maintained a rough orbit of a foot or so

around the professor, he caught sight of something that hit him with an almost physical shock. At first, he didn't see the whole thing, just individual parts:

Scalp ridged and bubbling with taut, smooth, and shiny scar tissue.

A lidless glass eye staring sightlessly from the puckered wound of its socket.

Two serpentine slits nestled in the concave space that may have, should have, once held a nose.

A gaping, lipless hole of a mouth.
Irregular, jagged teeth jutting at impossible angles from tar-black gums.

The one good eye, a merciless emerald resting in that blasted and burned landscape, looking directly into his.

It was the eye that did it. That one perfect eye, glazed with pity, was locked onto him. This time, he couldn't hold back the yelp that leapt from his mouth as he flailed backwards, kicking the desk out from under himself. His head cracked against the floor and fire shot up his tailbone from the harsh landing. His vision swam, blurry and unfocused, as he began to stand up.

Holy fuck! was the first thought to flash into his mind,

followed immediately by the good old mental daddy figure of the superego yelling at him. *How the hell could you do something like that?* the rebuke rang among the bells that had already taken up residence inside his skull. *It's gotta be hard enough going through life looking like that without some dipshit adding to it by acting like a freaked out little kid. Sure as hell better think of something to say now that you've gotten everyone's attention.*

Unsurprisingly, he had noticed that the lecture had stopped dead. The only sound in the room was the soft shuffling of sleeves against shirts and the light squeak of rubber soles across the tile. He didn't have to look to know that all eyes were on him for the second time in less than an hour. If it had been an option, he would have run away but he knew that he would see some, if not all, of these people again. Even if he could get a withdrawal from the class, he would come across the students or, more likely, the professor in some other class. He was going to have to do something or say something, but he had no idea what that would be.

He took a ragged, shuddery breath and opened his mouth to begin whatever pathetic excuse for an apology he could come up with before opening his eyes, too humiliated by his own stupidity to look into anyone's face. When he finally mustered the Herculean courage to look, he noticed that everyone in the room was indeed staring directly at him. That was to be expected.

He didn't expect to see them all standing in a circle, closing tightly around him.

They were moving slowly, methodically, silently. Gently moving desks to create a clear path, not jostling each other. No one was forcing their way to the front. There was no need to rush. He had nowhere to go. No point in discussion when they all moved with a single, unquestionable purpose.

He noticed, as he spun in lazy circles trying to make sense of the situation, that they all suffered some sort of grotesque malformation, birth defect, illness, or injury. The otherwise quite attractive girl with a cantaloupe sized pustule pulsing from her clavicle. An old man, somewhere in his seventies if the light wisps of nicotine-yellowed hair and rheumy eyes were to be trusted, with one stunted, twisted, liver spotted, and gnarled little hand growing directly out of his left shoulder. A legless man scuttling along on his fists. Conjoined twins with looped and wrinkled skin showing between the seams of their obviously self-altered clothing. A perfectly average, if haggard, woman suckling a baby with two forearms growing from its right elbow. Mangled limbs. Oozing sores. Flippers. Nubs. Scars.

Freaks.

The word flashed, unbidden, in giant marquee letters across the inside of his skull as a fist the size of a Christmas ham slammed into his gut, forcing the air from his lungs and a feeble wheeze from between his teeth. Thunder exploded from behind him and he felt a warm wetness grow in his crotch as his bladder let go under a sharp shot to his kidney. Something smacked into the back of his left knee and he crumpled to the ground. Another fist, bony and sharp as a stone, smashed into his jaw. He felt at least two teeth shatter from the force of the blow, sending bolts of lightning through the stars that erupted in his vision.

This is exactly how it should be, he thought, in a fleeting moment of lucid calm. *A place for everything and everything in its place. I'm finally learning mine.*

Someone roughly grabbed his hair, yanking his head back and pulling him to his feet. He found himself staring into The Eye again, the one that started the whole thing. That green gem floated serene, if slightly sad, amid the ruined face and a single tear rolled from a gummy, impacted duct as she swung the palm of her hand onto the bridge of his nose. With a crack that reverberated through him like the first shifting of an avalanche, he felt blood flow, warm and thick, across his mouth and face.

The steady pressure against his elbow released as the joint gave way, bending against probability and utility. The toes of his left foot were being pulped by the repeated pummeling of a hardcover Norton Anthology. The pressure at the base of his right thumb felt too much like teeth for comfort.

Jim had reached a point where the individual sources of pain ceased to matter. They were single, small voices from the bottom of a dogpile, photons on the surface of a star. Minute spaces between dendrites flooded with chemical signals and receptacles overflowing, the screaming of nerves became deafening to the point of numbness as he coughed blood and saliva into the air.

His mind separated, spinning off into its own realm. Lost in reverie, in remembrance of his favorite scene from an old black and white movie. Something from the director of the only *Dracula* that mattered, the one that sealed the end of his career. A ring of society's misbegotten: Midgets. Adults trapped forever in the form of children. Pinheads. Childish minds placed precariously atop the bodies of behemoths. Human torsos and other circus oddities (he was pretty certain a bearded lady was in there somewhere too). Grotesque accidents and cruel jokes of fate, birth, and genetics who, by no fault of their own, had been cast off from the care and kindness of humanity. Condemned to a life of pity in the best of situations, ridicule and outright torture in the worst. A mass of social rejects rolling and cavorting in the mud, calling out in unison over the cries of the woman in the middle. A simple chant. Repetitive. Three words that always reduced him to tears.

"One of Us."

With that same hand still hooked deeply into his hair, Jim took a moment to admire the deep, onyx shine of the recently waxed linoleum. From its inky depths, he could see his own face. Nose, smashed and contorted. Eyes nearly swollen shut. A deep indentation where his right cheekbone used to be. Skin ripped and exploded over swelling tissue. Jagged bits of teeth poked through torn lips that twitched and shuddered their way into a smile as his head was forced down to meet itself.

The Devil's Song

Sure. You can take my word or leave it. I don't have a say in something like that. Can't say I would listen to a lick of this nonsense, were I in your place. Ain't the sitch, though, and I hereby honorably swear that you are not neck deep and rising in a rushing river of my vocal fecality. Least not at the moment.

Hell, none of it was anything I expected noneways. I mean, Old Chuck wrote that ditty. A good enough one, fun and full of braggadociousness. I think someone even had it playing on the juke at Arnie's that night. Not a soul's foot wasn't set to tappin', neither. I wonder if He was the one? A slick joke, if true.

Either way, it was just a damn song. Nuthin' but the ramblings of some hairbrained hillbilly, regardless of how well turned his phrasing. Doesn't help his case that he seems to honestly believe that a race of alien lizard people controls every government. Guess he was the metaphorical broken clock.

Not a digital one, of course, but one with the hands and all. Preferably one so broken that the hands never move. Otherwise, the whole metaphor kinda falls apart.

No, I haven't taken my meds yet today. Who the fuck cares?

Whatever. Point is, I was over at Arnie's, just like every Thursday. Eyes practically floating in my skull from the JB. No. Before you start in, that doesn't explain any of it. Jerry was with me. Yup, he's a douchebag. And an idiot. Probably part Cherokee, too, but none o' that don't matter none here. He can account for it is the only part that matters. I mean, who disregards the words of *two* drunken fools, eh?

I was partway through workin' up a gal for the night. I may not be pretty, but my tongue is as slick as anyone's. I would have closed the deal if that red-haired asshole hadn't butted in. I ain't bitter, but ass is ass and, regardless of what I think of Agnes McConnigal come daybreak, she had enough to go around. All in all, I'd still give it a whirl.

The firecrotch put an end to that line of attack, leanin' in between us and talking about what a sportin' man he was. That I could have anything I wanted, so long as he could ask the same of me in the bargain. A simple wager. Winner take all and all that rot.

Now, some hayseed comes bustin' his ass into your game,

ragged mop of wiry red hair floppin' all over the place, yer bound to get a bit pissed at the fucker. Pullin' a fast one on that fool was just about the only thing to make up for it.

So I pulled him in close. Grabbed him by the arm straps on that stupid cliche pair of overalls, and leaned in real tight-like over by his ear. That's when I whooped out the loudest yes I could.

Now, this idjit, this flamin' moe-ron, he smiles real big at me. I mean REAL big. Damn mouth stretched like play-doh near meetin' in the back of his head. Teeth were just huge, bleach-white gravestones looming over us all.

And then he says, this dufus, he actually asks me what my game is. What's my game? Really? I mean, shit. Ya know? Shit. Boy didn't know what was about to drop on him.

It was karaoke night, you see. Jus' like every Thursday down at Arnie's. Most any night or day, really, so long as you had the guts to walk up there and a dollar for the juke. The stage was bare, looking a bit forlorn in the flickering light of a pair of old 100 watts. So I pointed right up at it. Told the fucker that he and his gold fiddle might maybe do okay up there, but so might me and my trusty Bee'trice.

I patted my right pants pocket when I tol' him this. The

deep one that Rainey done took out for me so that my dear lady could have a place. I still say that elementary music teacher got that one thing right. Ain't nothing make sweet music like the soft reeds of a good recorder.

You can take that to the bank.

I told him my price; an '81 Lincoln. Stretched. Black. Beautiful. Just the kinda thing to turn heads when you're rolling down the street, ya know? Chrome grill. Chrome Hubcaps. Chrome shift-knob. Whole thing had to be shiny. Told him I was sure a fine individual like hisself could get ahold of one easy enough. Just wanted to see it first. Just for laughs.

Damned but he didn't full out hyuck-hyuck at that one. Total belly jiggles and everything. His stupid fuckin hair just a bouncing and bouncin' around, like a star explodin'. But I heard a horn beep out front, right outside the big ol' plate windows.

Now, some bars don' like windows out front. People drinkin' there don' want nobody knowing their shame, I guess. So they black 'em out or just cover 'em up with junk. Arnie ain't that kind though. Like he says, this here's a free country and grown ass men and grown ass women shouldn't have no reason to be afeared of people seein' 'em gettin' a reasonable grown ass drink.

Doesn't hurt that the only ones around to look in are Murphy's cows in the field across the road.

So you can see out front just as easy as those cows can see in. This jet black, gorgeous beast positively glowed in the lights of the parking lot. And those rims, man. Those rims were like the bright light of heavenly grace. I could hear it speaking to me of love and the dear dreams born in its engine through the undulating pulses it emanates.

Ugh. I already told you. Can't take them on an empty stomach. Can I finish?

Thank you.

Of course, I knew it wasn't a one-way deal. He had to want something. Maybe my Chevy. You know, Blue. More likely my sister, though I don't know why he'd come at me for her. It's not a particular secret that she'd suck the siding off a trailer for a pack of Newports.

No, though. He rambled for a bit about ineffability and translucence and transcendence and how we don't need the things we don't use and some nonsense about photographs in the traditions of Innuits. Laid it on a bit thick, to be honest. As if I didn't know that the dude wanted my soul. As if I never watched the

Simpsons.

He offered to let me go first. All buck teeth and overdone bowing with a huge flourish of his arm, as if he was doing me a favor letting me set the baseline. I know that game. Everyone knows that game. Didn't matter.

I had him, regardless. So I took the stage, whipped out my 'corder and went to work, alternating between blowin' and singing. You've seen what I've got. You know I killed it. Jane Fergusson threw her skirt over her head at the half-way point. 'Course she'd been knocking back Beam since noon. There 'as no shortage of hollerin'. That's fer sure.

Had to give the shitkicker his run. Had to let him take his place. Even ended up having to let him borrow Bee'trice onna counta him forgetting to bring his own. I mean, what kinda Scratch doesn't bring his own instrument? Unprofessional, if you ask me.

The lights dipped further than normal. Say what you will about side effects and neural misfirings, but truth is truth and the place just got darker. Except him.

As the plastic met his lips, the most wondrous notes filled the air. Forget the mighty G, this guy-angel-whatever could work a woodwind. Even when no wood was involved. Ol' Bill was weeping. Ol' Bill, fer Christ sake! It was done.

I was done.

So he stepped down from the stage, hand outstretched. A bit about solid effort. Perhaps the effort was valiant. When I reached back, I stumbled.

Not an artful move. No grace to it at all. I hit the floor in a ball before unfolding flat on my back. Ever the gentleman, he reached down. Grasped my arm, and pulled me up into him.

Pulled the boot knife, the one I'd slipped into my off hand, and rammed it into his open flank. Right up under the ribs, just like dad taught me. Straight into the liver before slipping out and around the back to kiss the kidney. As his hands fell to the wounds, I swung around and up for a double poke in the throat.

He fell. I've got the prettiest car in town. I also know a new tune, if you'd like to hear it.

We've Lost That Wounded Look We Used to Have

It was back in June that I saw him. Twenty seventeen, maybe. It's been gone long enough that some of the finer points have gotten a bit blurry. Still, there are some things that never slip, no matter how loose the connections between neurons get.

The way the white burnt yellow in the firelight. The smell of old banana peels and cat litter and plastic and wax paper wrappers consumed in pyrotechnic chemical-physical reactions was overwhelming. Black lines fell into shadow. His shape was blurred in the flickering light and the fluttering of fur.

Just as it was meant to be.

The crackling of transitioning cellulose and carbon was loud enough that the drink-slurred mumbling was indistinguishable. The scrape-slip-scrape of rubber soles against macadam and the creaking of stiff leather didn't even register.

Oddly, what snagged us both was the acrid, acidic reek of Axe. I could feel my own nostrils flaring, oversensitive even in their restricted hominid state. His flew wide. Great, empty caverns drawing in the thick, humid city air and parsing the various compounds. I knew that my own could, too, if I was willing to shed this simple pale fragility, but I still wore that wounded look and couldn't mark the distinction twixt Apollo and Dark Temptation.

I could, however, blend back into the deeper shadows of the alley and become another vessel-burst drinker of cheap gas station wine. A regular haunt of the interstitial spaces between buildings instead of one of them. Avoiding the implied *we* meant quite a bit to me back then.

He didn't shift and scuttle, though. Didn't run to the dark when the scent hit, even though we all knew what it meant. His upper lip twitched and raised, just enough to reveal an overlong and pointed canine, and that was all.

"Ailuro," they chanted. One voice. One mouth. One, pure intent. "Ailuro. Ailuro. Ailuro."

Each time punctuated by a clang of aluminum on brick. Someone used to play ball. At least they wanted to. Maybe they never could quite pull it off. Maybe the pressure of that constant strain for paternal approval was what brought them to that particular alley on that particular night. Maybe they each wanted nothing more than to be something else, something more that they weren't allowed to be. Maybe that was tearing them apart inside until they had no choice but to tear something outside apart. Maybe none of it matters.

Because I can still hear the venom dripping from their jaws. It hissed when it hit the macadam.

"Furbaby."

"Fluff abomination."

"Violation."

"Bamboo-chewer," one of them spat, "will you finally look normal if we shave all that shit offa you?" The light of the trash fire gleamed a sickly yellow from the honed steel edge in his hand.

Because I can still see that same vomit hue glare from the burnished crosses on their chests. Twisted things. Warped symbols of good fortune in centuries long past. No one actually believed that was what they stood for anymore. They'd taken on an alternative meaning for nearly a century, despite the denials of history.

Because I can still feel my gut convulse. I can hear the doubts rattling in my skull. I knew that they knew. That I'd follow soon enough. That there wasn't a damn thing I could do about it.

Their words became a kind of growl of their own. Ululating, as if in chant, and blurring into an incomprehensible prayer for deliverance. I lost sight of him, eclipsed in their shadow.

I heard him first. Roaring over their pathetic imitation of his own wild intent, an explosion of noise that rattled the steel beams hiding beneath the brickwork around us. A deep, feral rumble of our shared past.

I want to say I saw him rear up, taller than all of them. Thick, muscled arms tipped with obsidian knives set to shred limp, bare, and pale skin. I want to describe the rivers of piss that flowed from them as they collapsed, and I want to say it all ended in commiseration and forgiveness and the sharing of pizza and beer and the growth of each and everyone.

Most of all, I want to say that I can't remember his howls; the final, pathetic yips of pain or the pieces of tattered fur and skin they held high, the reek of shit, and that one slowly twitching foot that stuck out from the circle. Their laughter.

What I honestly can't remember is who among us stepped forward first, or what we were thinking, exactly. I itched All over. An irritation that overran the terror flashing bright white strobes behind my eyes. I can't remember the stretching and the tearing and the bursting forth from within, anymore than I can remember the flavor of blood and bone. The sensation of sinew snapping between jaws of the high, desperate keening for mercy. Not for that time.

    I do dimly recall waking in the morning; as a slumped and sore naked mass piled together, sticky with the effluvia of the previous night. No less than a dozen eyes, none of whom carried that wounded sway toward the ground any longer.

When We Appear Before You Without Our Masks

There will be no compromises. We are not middle-class weaklings. Highly intelligent, we are the natural aristocrats of the human race, and steely-minded aristocrats never settle for less.

Those who oppose us will be exiled.

-Michael Swift, "Gay Revolutionary"

The lines were drawn up tight, rigid. Row upon row of men as far as he could see in either direction. Every one of them was broad-shouldered, thickly muscled. Even the many rounded bellies didn't hide that. Beneath soft curves, these men were *hard* and clad in nothing more than loose animal hide too rough to be called leather. The thick, tangled mats of their own hair was the only thing covering their chests and a good number of backs, too. They would never march to battle wearing more than that. Such had been sworn, on their own honor and on the bright steel they each gripped in their hands. Giant claymores nearly as big as the men who wielded them. Spiked maces and flat-ended mauls. Huge, pitted bundles of rebar welded together at their center.

Axes sharpened to a point that could shave the hair off a peach but would more likely split it in two.

Men who would never deign to hide their true selves again.

"Boy," the man next to him bellowed. "Stop staring around at all this flesh like a starving man before his last meal. I asked you a question. I hope you'll show more care when swinging that."

The man pointed a gnarled, calloused finger toward his weapon: a solid, oaken club bound in burnt black iron rings and five times the width of its handle at the end. The other men laughed at the care he took with its finish, oiling the wood until it gleamed golden in the firelight. They exclaimed the power of steel over wood and iron and told him he'd be better off using it as a cane, but he'd crushed in the roof of a discarded Cadillac with it and they'd stopped laughing. This wood would hold its own against their steel, he'd told them. The rings were just for character. The laughter that followed was different.

"I'm sorry," he said back. "Just lost in thought. What'd you need?"

"More like just plain lost." This man was thinner than the others around him, his beard longer and more flowing. Less bushy. He held a heavy, curved blade at his side, thick as a barely waning crescent moon, and a devilish grin shone in his almond colored eyes. The deep lines at their corners were the only things that belied his age. "I asked for your name. I'd like to know whose foolish swings I'll be dodging for the day."

"Benji," he replied, "and if I hit you, it's because you earned it."

"Benji, eh?" he laughed, loudly and deeply. "Fitting enough name for a cub bearing a stick."

"I'm no more a cub than anyone else here," Benji said, his clipped tone betraying the wound of the words. The words were too similar. Too close to the one time he worked up the guts to swing on his old man. *So, the little boy thinks he gets to act like a man, eh?*

"A few little whiskers on your chest and a horny old fuck slapping you on the ass don't make you a man," he sneered. Rich tones of a long-buried accent seeped through when he cursed. "But I imagine you'll get your first blood today. Then you'll be true of age and as ready for a real cock as any of those breeder bitches when they get their own first blood."

"I've had my share already, but I'd watch who you call bitches. The sisters bleed just as much and as often as the rest of us do and we need them watching our asses if we have to beat feet out of here."

"To hell with those b-,"

Longbeard was cut off by the blowing of the horn. Without hesitation or thought, ham-sized fists beat against barrel chests in time with their steps as they began their march forward. War songs filled with grunts and baying filled the air. Squads split up to march through a winding mess of roads, cul-de-sacs and dead-end streets that backed into and wrapped around each other. Peppered with squat ranch houses and simple, square yards.

"Fucking suburbs," Longbeard muttered next to him. Benji didn't bother mentioning how well he knew these particular streets. The little spot of forest down at the end of Ripple Street that had the best tree to build a fort in, squat with a thick trunk and heavy branches. Four separate generations of boys had fought each other over those property rights, each one immediately tearing down the old fortifications for their own superior design. The sad, crumbling shopping center with the unused parking lot in the back where everyone went to score a little weed or fumble and squeeze at each other. The old VA hall up the road from the firehouse that they all knew to keep clear of on Thursday nights when the Concerned Citizens committee meetings were held and plans were made for dealing with unwanted and unhealthy elements. Their motto, *Weeding the garden to promote better growth of flowers*, was his own old man's proud contribution to the betterment of society.

"What makes the grass grow?" The call went out, rumbling up from the rear ranks.

Benji's unit was half-way down a cul-de-sac and he knew they'd be breaking cover soon. The same way that he knew the formation they'd be in. For the same reason he pushed for his unit to take this quadrant. The Captain wasn't one for varying his strategy. He wasn't surprised to see the darkness behind the hedges down at the far end.

"Blood!" they answered as a single voice echoing off of aluminum siding and pastel lawn ornaments as they stepped in unison.

Behind the second house on the left, the one with the godawful lavender shutters his mother had always complained about, there was a flutter of shadow.

"Blood!" Slightly louder, with more of the rage they all held deep down behind it.

A soft thump from the garage on the right. The place used to belong to the Hendersons. He hoped they'd had the brains to bug out. Muriel always had a kind word and a glass of lemonade for him.

"BLOOD!" They howled into the air, the streets and, the trees. Windowpanes rattled with the force of it and the sky filled with birds as the breeders broke cover.

There were more than he expected to see, almost twice as many as were in his unit, but they were haggard. The man running towards him had eyes that were sunken deep into his skull and his greasy hair hung limply at his shoulders. He seemed barely able to lift the bedpost in his hand.

Big Jim was the first one to break ranks, running headfirst into the fray. He threw his three hundred fifty-pound frame onto the first man he hit. The poor sap was thrown to the ground as Jim began tearing into him with the steal claws he'd made himself. Blood spread in a pool beneath the two of them and splashed across his furs. The heavy copper smell was undercut by the earthier, rich, and sickeningly sweet stench as entrails tore free.

The weight of a collapsing tree crashing into his right shoulder brought Benji's attention back to his own surroundings.

That lanky bastard with the bedpost must not have had as hard of a time lifting his burden as it looked. He certainly wasn't having any trouble raising it up for a follow-up swing to Benji's head. Muscle memory inspired from months of training kicked in. He dropped low to the ground, just in time to feel the breeze from the clunky piece of wood blowing through his hair.

He lashed out with his free hand, directly into the kneecap. Benji had a flash of his father showing him just where to hit and just how to do it, so that what looked like an accidental foul would take an opponent out of the game for good. He pushed the image to the back of his head as pain lanced up through his arm and he realized he hadn't opened up his hand. Hit with his knuckles instead of the heel of his palm. Probably busted some of the knuckles against the solid bone, but he heard the telltale crunch he was looking for. Hollow-Eyes dropped to the ground, screaming, with his shattered knee unable to support his weight.

The spiked club pulled back over his shoulder almost of its own will. It wanted this. Begged for its first taste of crimson. Benji obliged, threw his full weight into the swing. He wasn't worried about an attempt to parry or block. This man was too wrapped up in his own agony to fight back.

His skull cracked on the first hit, the back caving in to meet the shape of the club. The spikes lodged in bone and it took more work to free it than he expected. Some of the older men had warned him about that, that those couple extra moments spent rocking it free could end up costing him his life. He quickly kicked at the man's head until the sharpened metal tore free.

Heart pounding in his chest, he took stock of his surroundings. No one was headed towards him, but three stood over Longbeard. It looked like one of them had knocked him to the ground with a brick to the head. A bright red gash gleamed over his left eye. The two swinging crowbars were kept just out of reach with wide strokes of that curved blade of his. One was limping and holding the side of his thigh when he swung. Even on the ground, the man was making them pay for every time they inched forward. But he couldn't do anything about the one with the bricks, just a few feet away. Another solid throw would daze him enough to create an opening for the crowbar duo.

Benji rushed over, taking advantage of Brick's preoccupation with Longbeard, and swatted the hand stretched out behind him. The brick held in it crumbled and the hand bent backwards, trailing bits of torn skin, muscle, and tendon. In a single, smooth motion, he redirected the inertia into a horizontal arc aimed at the face that was turning towards him. He didn't bother watching the man fall.

The one with the limp was bleeding out, slumping to the ground with a far-away look to his eyes that said everything. Confident that Longbeard could handle the last one on his own, Benji took a quick moment to scan the battle. Dear old dad's voice flooded his head. *Keep one eye on your surroundings. The guy in front of you won't be the one to crack your skull and drive you into the turf, it'll be the one coming around from the side or back.*

At a glance, it looked like chaos. Clumps of meat and metal, spraying red and screaming, spread at random across the yards and street. Then he saw the pattern he was looking for. The breeders had come out in more or less of a line, angled against the northwest corner of the cul-de-sac. They'd started out pushing hard and his own men had pushed back. Pockets of them were giving way, inch by inch, toward the houses. Benji's compatriots rushed into the openings, hacking, slashing, and smashing without concern, but it all looked too easy. A thought nibbled at the back of his skull.

The Captain's running a Counter.

His favorite play, a simple bit of misdirection any pee wee coach knew enough to watch out for it. So simple that not a single one of them had noticed it, not with heads running crimson with blood of scattered prey. Few drugs were as powerful as the desire to see your enemies driven before you. Especially when they had so recently been screaming for your blood, when you had grown up in the shadow of fear and they had been the ones driving you. That red haze burned out everything else, especially reason, and its siren song called for chase. They were playing right into his hands.

That meant something important was in the houses on the South side behind them. He looked over the yards and didn't see anything remarkable. No special reinforcing or ornamentation to designate stronghold or status given to an official of any sort. Not that the Captain would go in for that, anyways. *What kind of fairy needs a bunch of glittery froo-froo to show off?* He'd say whenever Benji asked for something nice, with the light glinting off the diamonds in his '84 State Champs ring all the while.

Benji hoped it wasn't children. They'd been told that all the little ones were clear, that several groups of children were intercepted while fleeing the area well before the siege started. All safe in the conversion therapy camps and far from the fighting by now. Of course, it wouldn't be the first time a general lied to his troops and it was far too easy to blame it all on bad intel after the fact.

It definitely wasn't the women. For all the old talk of chivalry, the rightful place of women, and high holy bullshit about the fairer sex being unfit for battle went out the window once the fighting started. It may have been desperation, or maybe the Sisters inspired some of them, but there were just as many of the ovarian-inclined in the streets brandishing fire pokers and kitchen knives and the odd chainsaw.

Then he saw a glint from behind an open second floor window. Sunlight reflecting off the curved glass. There was a bright flash followed by a loud crack that echoed off the houses. Jim's head vomited blood and brain onto the faces of the two women he was choking on the ground. His heavy body collapsed on top of them. Three more rang out in quick succession. Three more men fell.

Almost all the other men were too wrapped up in their own private battles to react. Benji looked back to Longbeard, whose curved blade was slicing through the crowbar bastard's throat.

Nearby, Tyriq was pulverizing the legs of some idiot who mistook his lack of a weapon for being unarmed. The sinewy muscles in Tyriq's calves and thighs worked like pistons, pulping muscle and flesh beneath his unshod feet.

"Sniper," Benji shouted as he ran to them. "Second floor. Middle window. Lime green house."

Both men moved immediately. They were already close enough to that side of the street to be out of the shooter's range of sight. Benji put two fingers to his eyes, then pointed to the large picture window next to the door. The curtains were down, blocking their view of the inside. Guards could be watching from the dark behind.

A garish, yellow stone frog lay in the overgrown grass in the yard. *Fucking Fergusons,* he thought as he hefted it onto his shoulder. He tensed his muscles, just like dear old dad had drilled into his skull. Breathed deep. Paused. Then put everything he had into launching it through the glass just as Tyriq kicked in the door. The curtains caught most of the inward explosion, but the noise was sure to buy them the moment of distraction they needed.

Longbeard and Tyriq were already inside when he got to the door. Two other men lay on the floor, leaking blood and moaning weakly. The heavy clink of metal against metal rang from the other end of the room.

The decades old football padding looked absurd strapped to his gaunt frame. Even more so with the faded brown and green helmet, faceguard patched with rust and fungus, making his head seem too large for his shoulders. Al Bundy reborn, channeling the glory of days long past. A washed-up idiot that couldn't tell when to let go.

The Captain.

Longbeard was laughing in large, booming guffaws, but Benji knew better. This was the same man who'd taught him how to weight an aluminum bat so that it looked normal and how to carry it so no one could tell the difference. There was no doubt in his head that the same bat was now swinging against the aluminum railing. No more than he doubted that it would hit like the wrong side of a runaway locomotive. The pads and helmet would provide a moderate amount of protection against his club and Tyriq's feet. Longbeard's heavy sword would shred them, but it would take longer than they could afford.

If you can't win, Benji could hear his voice echo from the past, *make them pay for every fucking inch. Make them bleed.*

Make them cry. Make damn sure they're thinking more about their shattered spine than victory when they leave the field.

"I've got this," Benji said to the two men in front of him. They stepped off to the right while he moved in a wide arc to the left, away from the wall, to the open side. Like any idiot would feel comfortable doing.

No words were spoken. The Captain would keep to his promise to never speak to his son again. Benji couldn't see his eyes in the shadows of the helmet. He wondered briefly if there would be anger there, resentment, pity, or sorrow. He wasn't certain what his own eyes were betraying, not that any of it would change what was about to occur.

He swept in, swinging his club low to block the inevitable shot to the knees. Aluminum and oak connected with a shock that rattled his gritted teeth. But Benji managed to redirect his momentum and knocked him to the side, pinning both bat and man to the wall. Tyriq and Longbeard saw their opportunity and took it, barreling past him and up the stairs.

Everything else in the world slipped away. The people bleeding and dying just outside of the house. The asshole with the rifle upstairs blowing holes in them. His brothers and their determination to stop him. This whole war. His worldview narrowed to two men with the weight of decades crushing them both.

Time fell back into place and he felt his hold on the old man giving way. Months of subsisting on whatever canned goods he had in the cupboard may have withered his frame, but he was still iron at his core. The same man who'd thrown Benji to the ground time and time again, screaming at him to get up the whole time. His grip slipped and he was thrown back.

Immediately, light flashed off the bat as it moved in a smooth backward arc, behind the back and over the shoulder into Benji's left collarbone. Something snapped and pain blasted brightly through his arm. The hand was numb, a lead weight beneath the agony. He almost dropped the club, but he forced himself to tense his fist through the pain.

What is pain? The voice he'd never hear again screamed in his brain. Giving up was a weakness that had never been allowed, even when he was a child. It wasn't an option now.

"French bread," Benji said, so light, it was nearly a sigh. The Captain was cocking his arms back, ready for the final swing to his skull. The one that would make it all go black.

He'd pulled back too far. Was too sure it was all done. Benji saw his shot and marked it. Despite the dueling pain and numbness in his arm and shoulder, he gripped the wood tightly and swung. Knuckles exploded upon impact. Both hands were nothing but shreds of skin and shards of bone past the wrist. Metal clanged as it hit the ground.

Benji always imagined, as he fought towards this moment, he'd hurl each slight, each screamed slur and thrown fist and that last rage-filled glare into these last blows. Instead, the few moments of praise sat just behind his eyes. Old images of this same face, round and red with laughter, overlapped the bitter, gaunt visage before him.

The crack of nasal cartridge under his fist when that pansy in fifth grade said... something. It didn't matter nearly as much as the lesson that needed to be taught. Two weeks at home helping fix the place up and his first beer followed. He aimed the arc low to the right, weight on his good arm, snapping bone and tearing muscle. Gravity enforced its will with a low thump.

The first time he'd crushed both legs on a quarterback while slipping during a tackle. At least, that was what the refs saw. The swing came underhand this time, hooking the faceguard on the spikes and tearing the helmet off his head.

A shelf of brass-gilded plastic trophies. An amethyst and diamond crusted white gold monstrosity of a state ring. Twenty ivy and brick institutions pleading full ride and praising his sportsmanship and sense of personal honor. Iron and oak hefted over his head. His back tensed and breath heavy in his chest, awaiting the last downward swing that would finish all of this.

Then it came. The night of his official signing. A half-drunk, slurred yell. Something about the TV he and Jason had to come out there to see. The rattle of the door handle, then time and the air around him turned to molasses. Clothes refused to leap from the floor onto the two of them. A hand that stubbornly continued to pump as the door flew open. Tendons released energy bound in muscles, bringing all of it down onto a screaming skull that had once been a man.

The Captain's body twitched twice. A sweet, retching odor of feces filled the room. Benji half expected to be yelled at for the mess on the floor, for the strawberry jelly and oatmeal that was soaking into the new carpet. Except that the carpet wasn't new anymore. It was faded, worn bare in patches and spotted with mildew. And it wasn't strawberry jelly or oatmeal seeping down to the padding under the fibers.

Benji slumped onto the couch in the corner as the adrenaline leaked from his muscles. Soreness was already setting in and he knew he would be feeling it in full force in the morning. He settled into an old, worn-in spot where the cushion cozied up to and around him. Just right, as the little bear was wont to say. The spot on his neck, right at the base of his skull, settled into the only angle he had ever found remotely comfortable. He breathed in the cloying, heavy stench of the room. Only then did he allow himself to look at what was left of the man on the floor.

No longer The Captain, the towering ogre spitting invectives while screaming for perfection. He was far too thin with pale, splotchy skin and knobby joints, shorter than he should have been. Just the man now. Just *a* man.

Benji waited for the big emotions to drown him. Rage. Resentment. Loss. He felt like he should be tearing down the walls like Sampson or wailing into the sky over a past that shouldn't have been, pleading for forgiveness or one last game of catch in the back yard. But none of it came. Not even the blankness of apathy or the cold hardness he had seen in some of the older men's eyes when they talked about the bad old days.

Just a soft haze of nothing.

After what seemed like hours, but was more likely a few minutes, he heard the stairs creaking under someone's weight. His muscles tensed and he gripped the handle of his club. Benji wasn't quite to the point of sprint or swing but was ready for either until a familiar laugh echoed down to him.

"That fucker didn't even put up a fight," he said as he came into view, pulling something sharp and barely off-white out of his tangled beard. The large, curved sword hung loose in the rope at his waist. "Just dropped his rifle and started begging the moment he saw real men with real weapons real close to him. Actually plead for pity, the damn fool. Like there's room for that anymore."

Another harsh, bellowed laugh forced itself from Longbeard's mouth. He stared at the shard pressed between his fingers.

"Tyriq's double checking the other rooms up there," he said, "but he won't find anything. They're all broken, in spirit or body, by now. From the window, I saw those that could lay down arms. The rest don't matter anymore."

Longbeard's thick, calloused hands grasped Benji's and pulled, leaving him no choice but to stand. The floor seemed fluid beneath his feet at first, something uncertain that would slide out from under him at any moment. His vision swam for a moment and his heart stopped dead in his chest. But the ground solidified quickly enough, the world coalesced into focus and his blood began flowing again. He was sure he hadn't betrayed this minor slip to the older man.

"I think it's about time we moved on, cub."

"Endless, He Said," previously published in *We're Here* (2024),
"When the Moon Sighs Solitude," previously published in *Subliminal Realities* (Lycan Valley Press, 2018)
"Under the Pretext of Propensity," previously published in *DOA II* (Bloodbound Books, 2013),
"The Glorious Adventure of The Premiere Size Queen of The Appalachian Trail Inside a Positively Gargantuan Cunt," previously published in *Queens of Death:Blood Reign* (Bludgeoned Girls Press, 2024)
"Interchangeable Parts," previously published in *The Ghost Is the Machine* (Post Mortem Press, 2012),
"What they Don't Tell You About the Mummy's Curse," previously published in *The Pleasure in Pain* (Dragon's Roost Press, 2024)
"Jesus of Jim Beam," previously published in *Bludgeon Tools* (Evil Cookie Press, 2020)
"Beautiful Things," Previously published in Shroud Magazine, 2009

Anton Cancre is an idiot and an asshole who desperately wants to find something positive in the world to hold onto. Generally speaking, they fail. Luckily, they look pretty cute while screaming and ranting a desire to burn everything to the ground and hugging all of you. Their luddite website is at antoncancre.blogspot.com. Pronouns: Any/All/Just Not Late for Dinner.

Check out other books by Bludgeoned Girls Press

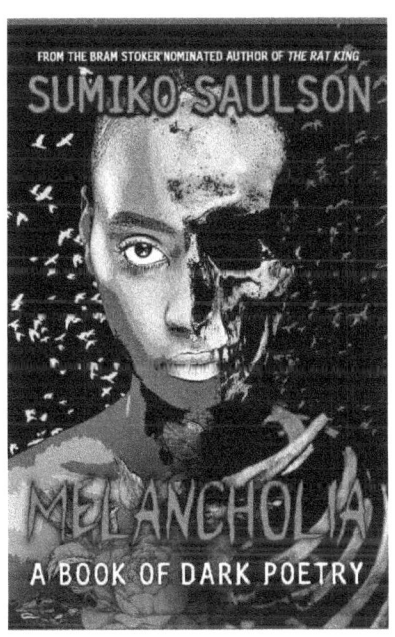